T0148674

MELCHIOR'S TALE

WORD TO THE WISE BOOK ONE

· ✚ ·

WARD MOTES

WESTBOW°
PRESS
A DIVISION OF THOMAS NELSON
& ZONDERVAN

WestBow Press books may be ordered through booksellers or by contacting:

WestBow Press
A Division of Thomas Nelson & Zondervan
1663 Liberty Drive
Bloomington, IN 47403
www.westbowpress.com
1 (866) 928-1240

ISBN: 978-1-4908-5710-7 (sc)
ISBN: 978-1-4908-5712-1 (hc)
ISBN: 978-1-4908-5711-4 (e)

Library of Congress Control Number: 2014918660

Printed in the United States of America.

WestBow Press rev. date: 11/13/2014

PROLOGUE

• ✛ •

And to think he had almost given up. He had even gone so far as to almost stay in bed that morning. After all, the sun was not even up yet. All that awaited him was the vast, bottomless darkness -- the kind of blackness that entombed the soul and numbed the senses. It was an insurmountable sea that pushed against the elder's aged body like the pressure of the deep itself, almost so that he could not even breathe.

But, he knew in his heart of hearts that the search must go on. That somehow, he must pull his body out of its grave-like slumber and search for light. That is what he had done since he was a young boy, search for light. But the days just seemed to grow darker and darker with no apparent hope of breaking the light of day.

"This isn't helping," sighed Melchior.

There was so much to do, so many preparations to be made. The night sky was waiting and it wouldn't wait forever. It wasn't like tomorrow night's sky would be the same. It was ever-changing, speaking different truths every night.

"No," he thought, trying to convince himself, "I have to be there. I have to see what God himself has to say about the days to come."

That was all it took. The elder magus was on his feet, a bit too quickly, probing the dark for his lamp. Then suddenly, light erupted into the room. The looming figure of a man stood towering over Melchior, enhanced by a brilliant light. For a brief second, he was transfixed, nearly awestricken. It was like all the stories he had read from the Scriptures, "Thus says the angel of the Lord" and so on. His body almost fell, overwhelmed by the epiphany before him.

"Master?"

"Othniel," Melchior answered, pushing past the sudden rush of disappointment.

It was his young confidant, Othniel, who had lived with the magus since his youth; although he was now a full grown man of thirty-something. The towering young man had become indispensable, acting as Melchior's eyes, ears, strength and courage. Without Othniel, the elder would have no way of going on.

"Thank you, my son. Where would I be without you?"

Where indeed?

"Everything is ready, Master. I let you sleep a little late. You seemed tired." Othniel replied, concern reflected on his lamp-lit face.

"Yes, I was." Melchior said wearily and then caught a second wind. "But, the night burns quickly and calls to us. We have wasted enough of the night."

Then, he put his wrinkled hand on the strong shoulder of the young man and finished with conviction, "Let us see what the stars have to say, shall we?"

The stars. That luminous choir sang the ages nightly for those who have eyes to see. They had always captured Melchior's imagination. For even in the busy city of Muza, the sky always erupted each night for all to see and the knowing to discern.

As the elder began his ascent of the stone staircase leading to the top floor of the observatory, his aged body stopped. He could feel Othniel's worried eyes bearing down on him. He had thought long ago that it might have been more prudent for him to live and sleep on the second floor as to avoid scaling these treacherous steps every night. But, that was before he had had the ceiling and most of the walls removed so he could see the sky better. Hind sight.

"I must..." is all he told himself and he continued on.

Why? It seemed a nightly question and almost always asked at the foot of these stairs. Why? Because of a vision. That's why. A dream. One which this wise old fool had carried with him since childhood. One that had sustained his family before him as they were driven from their homeland long ago. It was a calling, a destiny that had captured his heart as early as his first Passover, his first recollection of ever hearing about God's promise.

God's promise. That alone seemed the theme of every holy day and sacred festival his father had ever presided over. He could still see the tears in his father's eyes and hear the power in his words as he proclaimed from the high places what God had promised. A savior. A king. God with us. Someone to physically break the overwhelming darkness of this world with a true epiphany of God's omnipotent and holy light. Someone who would truly change the course of man's history. Someone to save us all.

But, at the moment, it all seemed as far away as his ancestors' homeland.

Finally, at the top of the stairs, Melchior paused only long enough to find a resting place. The actual observatory was small so everything he needed was within arm's length. With the absence of the ceiling and certain parts of the walls, one could easily see the whole of the sky over Muza. To the west, one could see the Red Sea and, to the northeast, the faint outline of mountains rose into view. But the terrestrial scenery was nothing compared to the stellar phenomenon arching the sky above.

"Now, this is where God shall reveal the mysteries of the ages, Othniel," Melchior said without even thinking.

To the orthodox Jew, only the Prophets and the Law reflected God's voice. But Melchior had come to find God speaking in the most unorthodox of places. His father had not approved. But, after the patriarch's death, Melchior had apprenticed with one of his younger uncles who had studied the skies with eagerness and a rabid anticipation. This new teacher saw no heresy in such things and saw God's handiwork in every light in the sky. He had, however, said that it was a temporary thing. That the day was coming when all that had been prophesied by the Law and the Prophets would shout from the sky and the One anticipated for so long would come. He said in that day the long awaited Messiah would be the revelation of God himself, and there would be no need to turn their eyes to the skies for answers ever again.

Melchior reflected on that thought with more than a little sadness. Not turn to the sky? He couldn't imagine it. But this was the Messiah, the promised one. If anyone could capture the elder's attention, it would be him.

He found everything he would need for his search on the table before him. Othniel, always the diligent one, had prepared it beforehand. And, even now, the gentle giant was busy laying out the scroll, readying it for Melchior to pen the night sky. The aged scholar wasted no time working out the preliminary sketch work. But, after a frenzy of symbols and strokes, he had to stop and massage his hand. The joints cried out, the pain almost unbearable. Tears welled up in his tired eyes as he cursed his hands for betraying him. It was getting worse. It was more work every time. He dropped his instrument, defeated, and not at all sure he could go on. He could feel Othniel's concern again as the dark world around him had begun to spin out of control with no hope of ever righting itself again. He tried to look at the stars, but turned away in shame. Maybe the darkness had won. Maybe this was the end.

No! This could not be the end. Not without His appearing. With this thought, Melchior bowed his head instead of raising it to the stars. He must always put first things first, he thought. The stars were not the issue, but the God that hung them was. It was not the message, but the voice of the one who sent the message. He had forgotten to call upon the name of the one who promised; The God of promise.

Calling out in the tongue of his ancestors, the aged magus vehemently prayed one expectant prayer after another. His cries were so intense that he found it hard to restrain his emotions. Overcome with a sense of sudden urgency, he began to plead with the God of his fathers that some good faith be shown the promises given so many generations before. As his weary voice began to give way under the strain, Melchior fell back into his seat, arms stretched to the heavens, fists clenched, and his whole body shaking. After a short while, his eyes began to reluctantly, fearfully, open as though they were afraid of what they might or might not see.

It was then, his eyes straining against an unknown light, that he realized this morning's sky was far different than any he had ever encountered before.

CHAPTER ONE

• ✚ •

The dream wasn't the first Melchior had ever had, but it was his last. For although he had many days left in his life, the elder never remembered having another dream. Now to most this may seem only unusual, considering his advanced years, but to Melchior it became a vast enigma for the rest of his days. For, you see, all of his nights since childhood had been filled with dreams and visions heavily burdened with meaning. Through much of his life, these nightly messages guided him along his way, protected him from danger and brought him vast success in all his ventures. For them to suddenly stop was a truly ominous sign indeed.

He may never have a chance to dream that particular dream again, but he would never forget it. It would both haunt and comfort him in his final days. For many years, Melchior had serviced countless souls by interpreting their dreams. It gave meaning to the senseless and order to the confused. The heavens always seemed to open to him with the proper answers, especially when the questions were his own. But, now he was stunned. He was left with a message that cried for interpretation, but the magus had no clue; nowhere to turn for the answers, or so it seemed. He was shackled to a mystery without a key -- a man with no direction. He was embraced by a dream that alone made no sense -- a dream totally devoid of meaning, if not for the star.

The star.

The dream began with the star. It broke the darkness with a brilliance that rivaled the sun. An explosion of divine power engulfing the darkness, overcoming it. The eyes of all men from the four corners of the earth now turned skyward. The heart and soul of mankind were given great courage and the faith of many was renewed. The star then descended upon the earth and came to rest in Israel. Its brightness subsided and left only the image of a man. Then the entirety of creation came and listened intently to the words of this man.

Until this point, the message of the dream seemed evident. Then, the image of the man began to shift and change. He took on the manner of a shepherd, staff in hand. His hair flowed a bit wildly to the shoulder, brownish with a touch of light. His hands looked worn from work, but his touch was gentle. The build of the shepherd was nothing special, but the way he carried himself revealed that the spirit of a true leader rested in his common frame. But his attention did not center on the leadership of a tribe, nation or people. On the contrary, the shepherd's deep dark eyes exposed a truly overwhelming compassion only for the care of the flock.

The flock was tremendous in number, but the shepherd knew them all personally. He took great pains to separate them from the other animals, shielding them from any possible harm. The loving eyes of the shepherd were always diligent, watching over the wanderings of the flock. His attention was especially taken by the newest arrival, a newborn lamb. It was not only the youngest and most defenseless of the group, but it was also the most innocent and unblemished. With a coat of purest white, it seemed at times to monopolize the vigilance of the shepherd. Toward the end of the day, the newborn had found its way into the powerful arms of the shepherd, a position it was apparently becoming accustomed to.

About this time, the shadows began to move. Strands of darkness came together taking the shape of an ebony lion crouched, ready to pounce. Its hateful, almost envious eyes watched from a distance as its hunger and boldness grew. The flock suddenly became alarmed and scattered in a multitude of directions, looking for shelter. It would seem, though, that their lack of faith did a great disservice to the shepherd. For the commotion did not go undetected by him. Strengthening the grip on his staff, he moved into a defensive position between the enemy and his flock. He did not, however, put the newborn lamb down first. This move only incited the predator to come in sooner for the kill.

Once again the image of the man began to shift, confusing the form of the shepherd with that of the newborn lamb. The two became intertwined, yet held fast to their individuality. The diligent love and leadership of the shepherd combined with the innocence of the lamb, causing a feeling of awe and sorrow within all who watched. The two mighty powers struggled for the fate of the flock. The man's image showed a calmer composure than that of the ravenous beast, leading one to believe that the defender would easily triumph. But the dark lion fought on, consumed with a hunger for the flock.

What happened next was all a blur. The black images of the enemy mixed with the illuminated form of the champion created a battle of light and dark. One could no longer make out the form of either combatant. The swirling mass began to pulsate, causing the light to overcome the darkness at times. And then, as the darkness exploded overpowering the light one last time, the images began to come into focus. Yet, 'focus' didn't seem an appropriate word for what Melchior remembered. For although the images solidified once more, the final moments of the dream seemed to make no sense.

It seemed as though the shadowy predator had won. The shepherd had fallen, using the last of his strength to fend it off. His final breath was taken with both hands clenched around his broken staff. The image of the man was still a chaotic mix of the shepherd and the lamb. Just as the strength of the shepherd had failed, the innocence of the lamb had practically given itself to the dripping jaws of the lion. Melchior remembered a certain sadness and overwhelming depression that turned to horror as the enemy began to hunt the flock. Their defender had fallen and the first kill had been taken. The rest of them seemed ready for the slaughter.

But, suddenly, the blackened beast found itself in a much bigger shadow. Turning, it saw the image of a man with his sword in mid-swing. But, by that time, it was much too late to react. With but one mighty blow, the darkness is dispelled and the dazzling light that began the dream exploded once more upon the scene. The image of the man then resembled the countenance of a king. Sheathing the mighty sword, the king now ascended his throne.

Voices empowered by heavenly energies broke forth into a mighty chorus, announcing a divine coronation.

"Holy, Holy, Holy is the Lord God Almighty
Who was and is and is to come.

Holy, Holy, Holy is the Lord God Almighty
Who was and is and is to come."

After several choruses, the volume became deafening, the aged dreamer reluctantly awoke.

CHAPTER TWO

◆ ✚ ◆

U pon awakening, Melchior found that his sleep had not been accidentally interrupted, but that it was Othniel who summoned him from the dream. The gentle touch of the servant's strong hands had apparently been moving the elder's small shoulder, forcing the magus to leave the strange, nocturnal message behind. To Melchior, he was a welcomed sight. For one thing, the sight of his large friend convinced him that he had not died, and that the dream was not a vision of the other world. Secondly, the two of them had always been together since Melchior had taken Othniel off the street and made him not just his servant, but his protector and confidant -- his friend.

The sight of Othniel's monstrous frame would stir fear in the strongest of men. Othniel's stature had made him an overwhelming presence ever since his youth. He stood a great bit taller than any of the other townsfolk, and, as far as Melchior could remember, he had never seen anyone to equal his strength. The behemoth's long, flowing hair was a deep blackness only equaled by the dark of night. Othniel wore his darkened skin like water vessels made from animal hide which were filled until they were tight and bulging. And, although most thought of him as slow of wit, his eyes revealed a great reservoir of wisdom only acquired by spending every waking hour learning from a magus.

The eyes of the aged wise man were a bit more than reluctant to open. The darkness had given way to the dawn, and the light was almost too much for Melchior's sleep-laden eyes. He could hear the noise of the city around him: the merchants pandering their wares; travelers moving about the streets; a couple of foreign-speaking sailors finishing up a rather heavy brawl; children chasing each other around the morning's traffic; not to mention a near deafening chorus of animals of all kinds and species. All of this he could tell even before his eyes adjusted to the blazing glory of the sun. The magi expected no less from the port city of Muza. For although it seemed to be eons ago when Melchior first set foot in the city as a young boy, it seemed to him as only yesterday that Muza was both much bigger in his young eyes and much smaller in actuality.

Muza had experienced tremendous growth during Melchior's long life. It was, and would almost always be, only a minor port city. It set along the southern Arabian coast of the Red Sea across from Ethiopia and just north of the entrance to the Gulf of Aden and the great horn of Africa. It was not established along the great caravan routes nor even the main sea routes. And it never aspired to any political power nor ever became the center of any vast kingdom. Despite all of this, Muza had flourished as a multi-layered society of holy men, merchants, kings, herdsmen, farmers and traders.

The uneducated traveler might come to the conclusion that the land of the Sabeans was merely a mountainous, desert-filled wasteland void of any possible life. But, upon actually visiting the land, one would find abundantly fertile slopes trailing into tremendous tracks of grazing land. Upon further investigation, it would be found that the people of this dry region have become experts at manipulating and harnessing what little water they found at their disposal. Vast irrigation systems unparalleled at this time ran from the mighty man-made dams (like the one found at Marib) or the multitudes of natural springs. The fruits of this ingenious labor were abundant and more than capable of supporting the growing civilization budding in Muza. Rice, dates, almonds, melons, aromatics and even some frankincense and myrrh were but a few of the cash crops that kept this region self sufficient. The frankincense and myrrh of this area did, however, pale in comparison to the quality of the spices of Oman and the Hadramant to the east.

Although Muza was surrounded by a multitude of farmers and herdsman, the real power brokers in the city were the merchants and the traders. They were responsible for whatever exports the town had and getting the products to the caravans or aboard ship. The port being situated along the Red Sea meant that a great deal of its imported trade came from Africa. Ivory, gold, exotic fruits and animals passed from the Ethiopian traders to the caravans. The Egyptian sailors, at times, would chance the treacherous journey across the Red Sea to bring their personal exports along with merchandise from the Roman-controlled Mediterranean. And still a few merchants came from India, bringing their silks, gems, silver and gold to bypass the stiff taxes levied by the caravan cities of Qana, Shabwa and Timna.

Melchior now stood looking over the city with a sense of great admiration. He felt, as many other Sabeans did, that he was living at the very center of the known world. Rome prides itself on being a vast political power, exerting dominion over all the other nations, but Arabia alone controlled the flow of certain spices and religious aromas that were necessary for the Roman's pagan culture to survive. This fact, coupled with the empire's military failure to either cross the Arabian peninsula or sail the massive Red Sea, had made southern Arabia a safe haven from the mighty empire's clutches. A number of Muza's residents were exiles from a multitude of origins including Egypt, Syria, Babylonia, and Jewish. They found here a harbor of safety far away from the marching Roman legions. In fact, this region had not known of war, nor would it become educated in it for many years to come.

The elder's thoughts had just begun to turn personal when Othniel hesitantly broke the silence. What the servant had actually said never really registered in Melchior's memory. All the old one could remember was that his thought process was broken off of one subject and awakened back to the previous night's revelations. For instead of turning his full attention toward his beloved friend, Melchior made his way past Othniel and started a bit too quickly down the stairs into the sanctum. Othniel followed, a combination of utter surprise and heart-felt concern crossing his face, trying desperately to stay close to his mentor in case he were to fall. To the servant's surprise, Melchior not only didn't fall but he bounded down the stairs as if he were younger than Othniel. Upon witnessing this, Othniel's pace slowed a bit as his master disappeared into the darkness of the sanctum. Never having seen Melchior ever with such vigor, Othniel began to wonder what could possibly be so important as to possess his master so.

Finishing the descent into the inner sanctum, Othniel followed the sound of a storm of activity. The noise brought him to the main study and the sight of his master in a frenzied search through the many scrolls that lined the wall. It seemed to the young servant that Melchior had become involved in an impassioned search for something he had apparently lost that had suddenly become incredibly important. The study looked as though a band of angry Bedouins had ransacked it. And Melchior showed no promise of slowing his crazed search. Othniel tried in vain to gain his master's attention, only receiving angry stares in return. He finally restrained himself and quietly went about the work of cleaning up behind his master's fury.

Othniel retrieved many scrolls from the study floor containing a multitude of subject matters. There were star charts galore, manuscripts of dream interpretations, Arabian and Egyptian legends and prophecies, and historical documents from all over the southern Arabian peninsula. But, the majority of the scrolls were Hebrew scripture, wisdom literature and Jewish interpretive studies.

Othniel had just become engrossed in a star chart dated from the night before when Melchior opened yet another scroll and said with a sense of discovery, "Bemidbar!" From his years of study at his master's side, Othniel knew the word. It was Hebrew, meaning "in the wilderness". He had heard it before, though, as if it were a title or something. The gentle servant wracked his brain as if he were being tested. *"Bemidbar...Wilderness...Think...Think...yes!"* It was scripture -- from the Law. The first five books, called jointly the Pentateuch, Othniel remembered with pride, were given the first word in them as titles. Thus, Bemidbar.

It was then that the elder sage began to read and speak from the holy words as if he were there speaking them himself.

"The oracle Balaam the son of Beor,
The oracle of the man whose eye is opened.
The oracle of him who hears the words of God,
And knows the knowledge of the most high,
Who sees the vision of the almighty,
Falling down, but having his eyes uncovered;

I see him, but not now;
I behold him, but not nigh yet;
A star shall come forth out of Jacob,
A scepter shall rise out of Israel."

As the elder's voice trailed off into silence, Othniel began to wonder if this scripture had anything to do with the star chart he held in his hands. But before he could venture to ask, his master said as if to himself, "A star," and, after a moment of meditation, resumed his chaotic search as if what was lost had not been completely found.

This went on for several minutes, causing Othniel nearly to forget the very reason he had awakened his master. He began once again to try to gain Melchior's attention while keeping a whole new set of scrolls off the floor. There had never been a time in all the years that Othniel had spent with the sage that he could ever remember having so much trouble keeping up with him. It was obvious to the young servant that something had piqued the very imagination of the ancient mind of his friend to the point of igniting a fire that now blazed in his master's eyes.

Upon making a third turn around the main table of the study, Melchior stopped, obviously irritated, shook his fists and, upon turning to his friend, said, "The answer is here somewhere, Othniel. I must find it!"

Othniel began to feel a great sense of compassion, seeing the amount of desperation and frustration on his master's face. Melchior had been known in the past to become quite enthusiastic about his interests, but whatever subject had grasped his attention this time held him in a massive, vise-like grip. Yet, somehow, Othniel had to find a way to bring his master's attention around to the message the servant had carried since before the elder awoke.

But before the compassionate servant could say a word, Melchior's attention began to drift away again. However, this time the magus' attention was not focused away from Othniel, but became directed at the stack of scrolls his servant had retrieved off the floor. Reaching out, his withered hands brought out one particular scroll and pulled it to him like it was his newborn child. After a moment, Melchior turned once again to the main table. Using one arm, he cleared it of several scrolls, and then began to open the scroll with a great deal of care. By this time, Othniel had become lost once again in his master's search, feeling that, quite possibly, the quest was now over.

As the scroll was opened, Othniel could make out the heading and became even more puzzled. The parchment that Melchior had retrieved was part of the prophecies of a former holy man of Israel, Isaiah. Othniel had heard teachings from these holy words before and couldn't make any sense of what possible relationship a deceased Jewish prophet had with the Gentile, Balaam or with whatever had transpired the night before. Despite the servant's confusion, Melchior read on silently with great diligence. The elder mouthed every word, gaining in confidence along the way that what he was looking for would be found within these sacred words. Then he stopped and re-read a section several times beginning to speak aloud.

"The people who walked in darkness have seen a great light;
Those who dwell in a land of deep darkness on them has light shined."

The ancient one's voice trailed off and his eyes began to wander toward the observatory stairs as if he were remembering the events of the night before. Othniel then remembered the star chart and Balaam's prophecy and his master's own words, "The star." Melchior was apparently gathering pieces to a tremendous puzzle and the key was the "great light" of Isaiah, the "star" of Balaam. Othniel, his mind racing, tried to remember any teachings that he had ever heard centering on these two scriptural stories. But where the servant failed to grasp the significance of the puzzle pieces that surfaced so far, his master began to put it all together as he continued to read.

"For to us a child is born, to us a son is given;
And the government will be upon his shoulder.
And his name will be called, Wonderful, Counselor,
Mighty God, Everlasting Father, Prince of Peace.

Of the increase of his government and of peace there will be no end,
Upon the throne of David and over his kingdom,
To establish it, and to uphold it with justice and with righteousness
From this time forth and forevermore.
The zeal of the Lord of hosts will do this."

Most of what Melchior had read became lost to his faithful servant. And the connection the had with the former information, Othniel left for later thought. For the word "child" awakened in him once more to the urgent message he was to carry to his master.

"A child, master! A child is being born!"

Othniel stopped short of continuing, seeing the same angry stare from his master, but this time the look was intermingled with a touch of intrigue.

"A child?" Melchior returned still, a bit confused, and showing a reluctance to leave his impassioned search.

"Yes, sir! Word came at first light from a messenger of Barak, the Midianite elder of the herdsmen who pasture just southeast of town…" Othniel went on until he realized his master had drifted off again. Yet, it seemed as though this time the servant had finally gotten through to his hard-to-reach master. For Melchior's once faraway gaze focused again upon his friend, and with a sense of sincere compassion said simply, "Barak?…"

Othniel could see now that his master was ready to hear it all as he continued, "Yes, my lord, Barak has sent for you in desperation. For, although he is due to become a father, his young bride may well become a widow also."

Othniel was ready to continue but he soon found that he had said more than enough. The words had no sooner left the servant's lips when Melchior turned away from his scrolls and began to move quickly toward the door. Then, as if an afterthought, the elder stopped and reached back for the "Isaiah" scroll. His movement, though, had been too quick, and his feet became tangled up, causing his frail frame to begin to fall. But, as in times past, Othniel was there to catch him and protect him from any harm. The tired eyes of the magus met the concerned eyes of his servant as Othniel once again broke the silence, "You were apparently up most of the night and probably didn't sleep well. Surely, we must postpone this journey."

The fire returned to his master's eyes as he said, "No! We *must* go! Whatever is happening to Barak may have something to do with what's going on. I feel in my spirit we must go! I will rest along the way. Get my cloak, staff and sacred incense, Othniel. I must pack some of these scrolls to view later."

Othniel obeyed, although in silent protest. He had learned to respect the decisions of his aged master, especially when he invoked the instincts of his inner spirit. Melchior had never had a wrong "hunch" before. Yet, Othniel became greatly concerned with the physical condition of his old friend. He was very certain that Melchior would die on his feet in service to his quest of knowledge and understanding. But, God willing, not today! The young servant gathered the incense along with some medicinal herbs. His master would need their inner healing. And, as he packed them in the traveling bags, Melchior packed several more scrolls.

This was all still confusing to Othniel. What had any of the messages on the scrolls to do with Barak's condition or the birth of his child? Was it another piece to an already chaotic puzzle, or was it simply a favor for a dear friend? Or both? The servants mind recled as the two left the sanctum following an extremely impatient messenger. The herdsman had already reached his camels and had begun to prepare for the journey when something darted from the darkness of the alley and fell, rolling to an abrupt halt upon the ground before Othniel and Melchior.

The "something" was a young boy, and he was being followed from the alley by two angry men carrying swords. Their intent was clear.

CHAPTER THREE

◆ ✦ ◆

O n the ground before them was the figure of a young boy. Although he was not quite young enough to still be called a boy, neither was he old enough to have truly earned the title of man. Melchior, of course, felt such a title was an honor to be earned by experience and example of character. Yet, anyone could see that this "child" was about to grow into a good portion of manhood, but not for awhile though. For on the long frame of this soon-to-be man rested the face of a cherub. His dark hair flowed like wild rivers. His eyes were black pools of pitch that pierced the very soul. And his features, although soiled, bruised and bloodied, still possessed an almost graceful form.

His clothes, though torn and dirty, betrayed a bit of wealth, and suggested the position of lord rather than vagabond. The hands of the boy were not calloused, leading one to believe he had never known hard labor; and his feet were only recently bruised and scarred, causing one to think he had once work the shoes of sonship and authority. The features of his face, although childlike, were chiseled, sharp and strong. He was definitely not of local descent, for his skin, though tanned in some areas, revealed a paler hue in others. Whoever this young man was, he was not a beggar and he didn't belong here in the streets.

Emerging from the darkness of the alley behind him were two roughians intent upon capturing him and more than likely doing him great harm. Both were exceptionally hard to look at, considering the many scars, cuts and bruises each had. Their clothing was a swirling mass of differing colors, fabrics and international styles. But unlike the young boy, their clothes did not fit in size nor did they seem to fit the apparent character of the blade-carrying thugs wearing them. But it was certain bits of clothing, the horrible absence of at least one finger and the unmistakably repugnant smell of fish and the sea gave these cutthroats away as sailors, and as far as Melchior could tell, sailors in the most ill-reputed sense of the word.

For what seemed like an infinite moment, none of them dared to move. Then, suddenly, the boy uncoiled like a cobra and bolted like a scared animal. The two thugs pursued him, forgetting about the two observers. It was then that Othniel intervened, catching the young boy with his left hand and the arm of the first cutthroat with the right. Amazingly, Othniel had him disarmed and heading uncontrollably into the other seaman in the blink of an eye. By this time, the messenger had had enough and had drawn his own sword. Determined to take matters into his own hands, the herdsman prepared to dispense justice on the spot. But the self-appointed executioner soon found himself sword to sword with a third individual, who had appeared suddenly from the shadows of the alley.

With every attack of the angry herdsman, the swordsman gained the advantage. It was obvious that if he had wanted to run him through, he could have done it. But for some reason, he held back and simply disarmed him. Then, the victor stopped and turned toward Othniel and Melchior. Othniel found himself struggling somewhat with the wiry youth as Melchior assumed a defensive pose behind his walking stick, as if he were actually going to join the fray himself. And just as it seemed physical confrontation was inevitable, the swordsman sheathed his sword and removed the cloth that had covered most of his face.

"Othniel! Melchior! What a pleasant surprise!" said the swordsman flashing a killer smile that was half charismatic, half sinister.

"Ah! I see you have caught my little street rat. I am forever in your debt."

Their attacker turned out to be a clean cut man in his thirties dressed much like the other two thugs, only cleaner. He sported a nasty scar along his left cheek and was missing a few teeth. He was a well-fed individual with sleek, attractive muscle tone. His hair was not so much short as nearly non-existent; and as he removed his turban, he revealed a surprisingly handsome head to the heat of the morning sun. Affectionately caressing the gold and jeweled inlaid sword he had just put away, this smiling Arabian sailor's every word was surrounded by an air of arrogance and mischief. There was only one word for this man.

"Bassam!"

CHAPTER FOUR

✦ ✚ ✦

"**B**assam!" Othniel finally said, clenching his fists and nearly hissing through his teeth. The gentle giant Melchior had raised and come to love had become transformed somewhat into a mountain of pure rage and hate. The look in his eyes told the tale, but also kept its secrets. For although it was obvious, even to the struggling young boy, that there was some great animosity between Othniel and this 'Bassam' character; there was no clue as to what had caused that animosity. Othniel had just reached to the ground with his one free hand and picked up the messenger's dropped sword when Melchior stepped between the two potential combatants, giving his angry friend a stern, but understanding, look.

Melchior continued giving his protector a deep, probing look, digging down into the core of Othniel's being and soon finding a calmer, gentler, almost broken side to his previously enraged friend. After a moment of deafening silence, the magus spoke in a clear, even tone, as to not be misunderstood.

"Now is not the time, and this is not the place, my friend," he said lightly touching the tense shoulder of his enormous ally.

Melchior then reached over carefully to Othniel's left hand, never breaking eye contact and said, "Let the boy go. You are hurting him."

Othniel hadn't realized how tight his grip had been on the young boy. He dropped him immediately upon seeing that he had twisted the boy's tunic tightly around his young throat. Once on the ground, the boy began to gasp and cough, not realizing himself how much the giant had cut him off from his air supply. Othniel turned away from Bassam, half in rage and half in horror and fear of what he was actually capable of under the circumstances.

Bassam, whose very name means "smiling," was being very true to his namesake, once again grinning from ear to ear as if he had accomplished some great feat. The young boy had finally come to his senses and at once thought of running, only to realize that all of his exits had been cut off by Bassam's thugs. Othniel refused to even open his eyes, which were shut vise-like in pain and anger. Melchior stepped right up to Bassam in an almost challenging way and began to speak very cuttingly to the sailor.

"So you have reduced yourself to chasing children through the streets with swords? Now, what is next? Threatening the elderly widows with clubs?"

Bassam almost laughed at the thought and gave a snide little half-smile in response.

"What possible business could you and your" (he hesitated to say it)"*men* have with this young boy?" Melchior finally asked expecting a lie in response.

"Melchior, my dear friend," Bassam began through that wicked little smile of his, "it is simply business. The boy's father booked passage upon my vessel."

"His first mistake!" Othniel said, still facing away from the others.

"He paid half the fare up front," Bassam continued, ignoring Othniel (or at least trying), "and promised the other half upon completion of the trip. I was suspicious from the first, considering this questionable promise. You see, once we entered the port of

Muza, the scoundrel was, of course, found without funds. Robbery, he claimed (humph). It was obvious that this man was no better than a thief, and never intended to pay me my fare."

"Liar!" snapped the young boy, who Melchior had thought mute until now. "You lying dog! Your men stole my father's gold and then you killed him with your own sword!"

The boy was using a dialect native to the Mediterranean. It was thick, and the boy was talking too fast and flared with too much anger to be perfectly understood. But Melchior needed only watch the boy and know Bassam's nature to realize what he was saying.

"Oh, my, my! It is a terrible thing when a father involves his son in such a scandalous treachery, isn't it?" Bassam said, not bothering to look for agreement amongst those around him. "When I confronted the man, he drew a sword on me and my men. He challenged me on my own ship. I had to defend myself. Unfortunately, the child's father was not as good a swordsman as he was a liar. Oh, I suppose he wasn't that good a liar either," Bassam finished with a muffled smile.

"You spawn of Hades and Des the Deceiver! That you would call any other man a liar is an abomination!" The boy now stood as if ready to pounce on Bassam himself.

"Well," Bassam said, as if offended, "the child has a rather colorful vocabulary, doesn't he?"

"My father," the youth continued, "I'll have you know, was a respected delegate of the Senate of Rome and was on the Emperor's business." He then cut himself off as if he had said absolutely too much. Now the boy had everyone's attention. Even the messenger who had not picked himself up off the ground seemed a bit more attentive. Bassam even seemed shocked, for once. And Melchior, who usually had an answer for everything, was astounded.

Was the boy lying? Was he, in fact, the son of a Roman delegate? All the evidence seemed to point that way and Melchior was definitely not going to take Bassam's word over the boy's. One could read Bassam's thoughts all over his scar-ridden face. He was apparently wondering what this new bit of information was going to mean to him financially. There was more silence and then Melchior began to try and change the direction of the conversation.

"Bassam, this boy surely can be of no use to you, being so young and frail, and seeing that he is not accustomed to hard labor. Release him to my custody and he will be taught a better life."

Bassam's look went from confusion to ambition as his smile returned and he replied. "Now, Melchior, you know that in the absence of any other barter, the child is legally my property for proper payment of my fare. Anyway, the child has displayed a unique educational background that might bring a good price amongst the scribes of Egypt or you brethren in Babylonia."

Melchior now realized that if he were going to keep the boy from harm (in other words, away from Bassam), he was going to have to pay. He began to feel a bit like he was repeating history as he prepared to barter with the questionable business man.

"What is the price, Bassam?" Melchior asked as Othniel reacted violently.

"What? You can't seriously be thinking of dealing with this cutthroat!" Othniel was now turned back toward the others and his rage was quickly returning. Melchior caught his friend by the arm and battled once more for his attention. Othniel only dared to glance at his mentor, knowing he would have to back down again. Frustrated, he turned and stepped back toward the sanctum door.

Melchior turned back to Bassam, who seemed to be adding the cost up in his head and must have just hit the total by the look on his smiling face. There was a moment of mental adjustment, and then Bassam opened up like one of the bazaar salesmen.

"It seems to me that the last time we did business together, I came out on the shorter end of a bargain."

Melchior would have argued, considering real history, or a small thing called truth, but decided against it.

"Figuring that, with this youth's educational background, and the going rate of the day," he looked up as if he were reading the heavens and began to count his fingers, "four times what you paid me before."

Othniel had finally had enough and turned once again and started toward Bassam, almost knocking Melchior over in the process. "You devil!" Othniel said, tightening the grip on his sword. "You thieving, lying, greedy devil!"

Bassam began to back up as Othniel began to get a little too close. Unfortunately for the seaman, he wasn't watching where he was backing and tripped over some discarded trash. Now Bassam's smile was gone as Othniel stood over him, contemplating his next move. But that wicked little smile soon returned as Bassam's men set the blades of their swords along both sides of Othniel's large neck.

Picking himself up, Bassam said, with a sense of arrogance, "I believe the price is now five times." He then gave Othniel that accusing look and that snide little half-smile before attempting to dust himself off. Othniel actually thought about taking them all on at once but was interrupted by his mentor's voice.

"Pay him, Othniel," Melchior said, betraying a tone of defeat.

"Yes! Pay the man, Othniel!" Bassam said, half way mocking Melchior as he waved off his thugs.

Othniel reluctantly pulled a pouch from a hidden pocket in his outer robe and began to count the gold pieces. The amount was set and Othniel didn't have to ask. He would never forget the price paid to Bassam before -- never! Bassam hadn't forgotten either and began to follow the count more closely until he realized with a clever little smile that the pouch held not only five times the original price, but five times that. With a nod, Bassam's men began to position themselves as their leader's greed grew. Bassam began to fondle his sword handle anew, fingering every jewel several times. And just as Othniel finished counting, he realized that the price had just gone up drastically. But, before Bassam could "re-negotiate" the deal, they were interrupted by the sound of approaching hoof beats.

Two magnificent stallions broke into the street, coming off a full gallop. Their riders drew swords and one of them asked, "Is there a problem, Melchior?"

The tension thickened as the horsemen waited for an answer. Bassam's men froze, and Othniel was almost afraid to speak. These were two of Barak's men, come to encourage a hasty departure. By the look on their faces, they completely understood what was transpiring here.

Bassam took the gold from Othniel's hand and said, "No problem! Just finishing up a small bit of business." The smile on his face was tense and insincere as he turned to Melchior. "Nice doing business. Our paths seem destined to cross, Melchior. God be with you until they cross again."

Coming from Bassam's lips, this cordial farewell became blasphemy. The conniving devil flashed his half-cocked smile and disappeared down the same dark alley from which he had. Once out of sight, the boy collapsed onto the ground out of pure exhaustion and glorious relief.

CHAPTER FIVE

· ✚ ·

T he midday heat suggested to the boy that he had been unconscious for several hours. He looked behind him, but saw no sign of Muza. He checked ahead of him and saw a near wasteland. Under him was a moving camel packed with water and supplies. Where was he? Where was he headed? And why? These were just a few of the questions swirling around in his bright, young mind. His confusion was suddenly interrupted by what he thought to be an awful wailing sound. As he turned toward the noise, it turned out to be the old man (Melchior he thought his name was) singing in a traditional mid-eastern style. The words to the "song" were foreign to the boy, who wasn't sure if he could have understood the old man even if he sang in Latin or Greek. He must have stared at the magus for quite a while when another voice startled him from his hypnotic stupor.

"It is Hebrew. Part of the Psalms from the sacred writings of King David."

The boy turned so quickly he almost fell off his camel. But, before he could even begin to fall, a large hand caught his shoulder and straightened him back up.

"Careful, young one. There is no need to be afraid any more."

The youth found himself eye to eye with the giant, Othniel, and suddenly he became quite concerned. This stranger's size was still a great deal more than intimidating, yet something about his eyes had changed. The fury and the rage were gone and had been replaced with a look of peace and a depth of feeling that the young boy could not quite explain. Compassion filled every look. Understanding swelled in every movement. Suddenly, he felt very much at ease. Finally, he decided to trust the two of them, especially considering the price they paid to free him from that scavenger, Bassam.

"It seems I owe a great debt to the both of you." His voice trailed off when he realized that the three of them were flanked by four horsemen dressed in a layered sort of garb. He recognized some of them from the confrontation with Bassam, but wasn't sure who they were. Before he could ask concerning these armed guardians, Othniel broke the silence once more.

"You only owe the master your life! Considering the amount of gold he just paid out for your freedom, and the fact that your young life would have been over in the hands of that tyrant, yes, you owe him a great deal more then you will ever be able to repay, boy!" The rage was slowly returning to the gentle giant's eyes as the conversation had turned a little more personal than necessary.

"Stephanus," the boy ventured to say, almost afraid to speak.

"What?" is all Othniel could say.

"Stephanus," he repeated, almost whispering. "That is my name. Not *boy*."

"Stephanus," Othniel said acknowledging the boy's comment. "You *are* Roman. So, is it true your father was a delegate of the Senate?"

"Yes," Stephanus said, wiping a pool of sweat from his brow, "and, I hate to sound ungrateful, but it is important that I return to Roman soil as soon as possible."

"Impossible," Othniel said, as a matter of fact.

"What?! You don't seem to understand the importance of my return! You simply must get me back to a Roman controlled providence! At once!"

Othniel began to get irritated again, yet held his composure. He tried to speak in soft, even tones, but was betrayed by a cutting, angry rhythm.

"Impossible. Were we still in Muza, most of the sailors in the area favor Bassam, and a journey over the caravan route is out of the question. Melchior would never survive it."

"Take me to the caravans and I will travel alone to the empire!" Stephanus was almost over his shyness and was beginning to reveal an arrogant, almost spoiled side of his personality.

"Of course! And have you end up in the hands of someone worse than Bassam? I think not!"

Stephanus' first thought was, "Worse than Bassam? Is that possible?" But he decided not to pursue that line of thought. Instead, he asked, "Where in the name of Zeus are we going anyway?"

"We go nowhere in the name of Zeus, boy." The singing had stopped and Melchior had joined the conversation.

"My name is Stephanus and I never meant to challenge whatever god or gods you and your friend here serve. I just want to know where we could possibly be going in this…this…wasteland?"

Melchior stopped his camel and gave Stephanus a stern, angry look. And as the rest of the camels came to a halt, the elder composed himself and said; "We have been called to the side of a dear, old friend, who is both living his last days among us, and is about to become a father for the last time. Both acts of life and death require my attendance as the representative of the Most High God among these people. Stopping to save you may have already robbed me of my chance to deliver glorious news to my dying brother, Barak. Not only that, but our hesitation may possibly cost the new mother and her child their lives. That being said, not only do you owe me a debt of gratitude, but you may well owe your life to a people who you never knew existed. That, Stephen, is where *we* are going!"

This bit of information took the boy totally by surprise. So much so that he could hardly even whisper, "My name is Stephanus." Not that anyone was listening as the group continued on. He was terribly confused about a number of things now. Who was this Barak, and what was the 'glorious news' Melchior had for this dying man? Would they be on time, or would all this tragedy truly be his fault? And who was this 'Most High God' Melchior 'represented'? And, Stephanus still wondered what past dealing Melchior, Othniel, and Bassam had had. But all this had to be tabled for now as the small band of travelers topped a high place and their destination came within sight.

CHAPTER SIX

◆ ✚ ◆

A s the troubled party came within view of their destination, just peeking over the horizon, the encampment itself didn't look like much. But once over the peak, they could see that the tents went on for miles. The encampment was arranged in a crescent shape centering upon a group of wells. Surrounding most of the settlement was a mountain range that trailed into rolling hills that finally phased into vast lush pasturelands. From where Stephanus was standing, he could make out the manmade, complex network of irrigation ditches, which seemed to extend from the mountain down into the pastures. In fact, it seemed that this near picturesque carpet of green was owing to these water funnels for its very existence.

The camels had stopped, as if they were also frozen in awe. Yet, the word 'awe' did not even come close to explain what was going on in the minds of these travelers. Othniel had topped this peak many times, and yet he never quite got used to the sight before him --a sea of white, pulsating with abundant life, overflowing onto a green valley with wealth and divine blessing. A tear tracked Melchior's sand-blown face as he began to contemplate the task that lay before him. And Stephanus, although somewhat taken with the view, had just gotten his first whiff of the multitude of animals that covered the valley.

While shielding his face from the stench, Stephanus noticed the movement that pulsated through the whole encampment. He had seen Roman legions before, and with them, the activity of war and death. But he realized a great difference here. Instead of the regimented rhythm of armies and subordinates, life was on display here. Children played. Herdsmen tended their animals. The women of the camp gathered water and went about the domestic work of the day. Animals of all species moved about the grazing land. There seemed to be an infinite movement in, out and around about the entire settlement.

Part of this movement included another small caravan of camels and horsemen that had stopped along what seemed to be the main set of tents. This group had caught Melchior's attention also. The elder began wondering what area these visitors hailed from. For, it seemed that the more he looked, the more familiar this group of strangers appeared. Melchior had moved up for a better look when the lead horseman got in front of him, stopped short of the ledge and let out a yell that filled the valley. There was a pause, and then someone returned the call. The messenger who had led this party from the first turned and said, "We are not too late after all! Our master lives and his young bride is still in the pangs of birth." A collective smile broke out amongst the party as all their hearts were lightened.

All, that is, except Melchior, who replied, "Very well, then, let us make haste! The Lord's work is before us!"

With this, the aged master let out a yelp and he and his camel took off straight down the path that led to the tents. Othniel almost fell off his camel reaching out in concern for Melchior. These outbursts kept Othniel greatly concerned for his mentor's health and well-being. Even now, the gentle giant was in pursuit of his teacher with a great concern and diligence.

As welcoming parties come, the one awaiting them ranked rather poorly. A handful of herdsmen and a couple of Barak's oldest sons were all that graced the entrance of the main tent. The leader of this rag-tag bunch was a bearded, middle-aged herdsman who had just welcomed the group of foreigners. And by the look on his face, he had held his peace as long as possible. Just as the last visitor had disappeared within the tent, and Melchior's party was still a ways off, Barak's oldest son, Massoud, finally spoke out, "By all that's holy! How can father welcome these squatters into his tent at such a time as this!"

His younger brother, Sayed, shuddered at this outrage and replied, "Massoud!" he said in a hushed but stern voice, "Have you no respect? Those men are guests of our ailing father. What if they were to hear you -- if father were to hear you!"

Before Sayed could utter another sound, his brother burst in defiantly, "These *guests* are nothing more than thieves and vagabonds! What do I care of what they think of me? They know how I feel! As for father, I would be surprised if he could hear his own voice, much less me. Besides, when was the last time he ever really listened to a thing I said?"

Massoud was beginning to get louder as his face got redder. His usually handsome profile began to distort into a twisted vision of the hatred his heart had held for so long. He remembers when this whole valley belonged to his father and his father's people. It had been passed down from generation to generation. And now, the time was nearing for his father to pass it on to his oldest son, him. Only problem, there was less of the land and more and more of those... those Hebrews. "Those exiles," he began, "have nearly taken over the north end of the ridges. And every year their numbers increase. Yet, father grants them almost every wish, believing there to be a kinship between our two peoples -- a family relation between our two tribes."

Massoud had now stepped to the side of his obviously nervous brother and began to talk in a more personal tone. "And, adding insult to injury, father has done the unthinkable! To think he actually took one of *them* as his wife. And, now, in his old age, that Hebrew dog is bearing him a child! Heaven forbid! If the child lives, our people will be forever linked by blood. What shame that would bring to our camp. Think of what dishonor this brings to our dear mother's memory."

Sayed broke in, trying to calm his irate brother, "Massoud, you know that father hasn't done, and would never do, anything that would bring shame to our clan."

Unfortunately, Sayed had grown accustomed to being interrupted, especially when Massoud was on one of his tangents.

"Hasn't he?" Massoud said, cutting his brother off. "What if *it's* a boy? Will you share *your* inheritance with him?"

Massoud said this and stormed off, fuming. Sayed wasn't sure how to answer him, but he guessed he would share -- out of respect for his father, anyway. Sayed mulled the question over a bit and then was awakened from his quandary by the cry of the messenger. The holy man had arrived! He had always respected the wisdom of Melchior, even rivaling his respect for his own father. And, now, during Barak's last hours, the representative of the Most High God would be by his father's side.

Massoud had heard the cry, too. He turned back to witness his younger brother returning the call with a shout of hope. A scowl returned to his already tensed face as his eyes narrowed with disdain and his mouth pursed with a quiet displeasure.

"Wonderful. Just wonderful! The cast of his crazed tragedy is now complete. The play can now begin," Massoud said, waving his arms in mockery. "A senile *patriarch* on his death bed. His Israelite concubine giving birth in an adjacent tent. A child that should never be born! And, now!" he hesitated with that sense of dramatic pause, "And, now, we have the magician and that monstrosity. How much insanity are we to endure this day?" Massoud said, looking at Sayed, "How much more are we to endure?"

30

For the first time in his life, Sayed was truly afraid of what his brother was capable of. Massoud seemed to contradict himself in every word and deed. He spoke of honor, yet he disrespected their father with every repugnant word. He spoke of insanity, yet became more irrational by the minute. He spoke of monsters, yet it seemed to Sayed that Massoud was the one proving to be inhuman. And, he had spoken of tragedy. Sayed hoped they could avoid the pitfalls that lay ahead for them all.

Chapter Seven

◆ ✛ ◆

By the time Othniel, Stephanus and the horsemen made it to the tent entrance, Melchior was already being helped off his camel by a couple of large men. Othniel wasn't sure the men who had come to Melchior's aid were as able or as careful as they needed to be. So, by the time the aged mentor touched the ground, Othniel was there to brace him. Melchior had gotten so used to this that he really never concerned himself with falling or being injured. He had learned to rely on the care of his large protector. And with good reason.

Sayed was the first to officially greet them as they got their bearings and began to make their way to the tent. The rugged herdsman greeted Melchior with a familiar embrace.

"Thank the God of our fathers! You've arrived just in time."

Melchior wasn't sure he liked the sound of that comment. His concern had been mainly with Barak, and, of course, he thought of him first.

Sayed continued, "The child is being born even as we speak and the mother is in need of your assistance." Then he said, regrettably, "The child is not delivering properly. We have begun to fear for both of their lives."

Melchior now found himself torn between two greatly urgent tasks. The dilemma before him was so great that it left him both speechless and indecisive for the first time in his long life. Which was more urgent? The death bed of his dear friend, or the possibilities of a fatally difficult birth? He had apparently taken longer than usual to make a decision, for Othniel had decided to break in, "Master? What are we to do?"

Melchior looked up from his thinking with weariness in his gaze, and said, "Othniel, I believe we must rely upon your eyes, your hands and your knowledge to see the young mother through this crisis, for in most of these cases I am physically your inferior. What's more, I must go to the side of my friend. I have news that cannot wait."

Sayed gave Melchior an astonished look, as if that were not quite the reaction he expected. But he knew that the elder would neither put the child nor the mother in any undue danger. And, despite his astonishment, Sayed respected the word of the magus unquestionably. Othniel felt a bit of hesitation, showing a great reluctance to leave his master's side, and yet he had even more respect than Sayed concerning Melchior's decisions. Stephanus had become a quiet spectator in the first act of this drama, yet as Melchior voiced the words, "Take the boy with you," he became quite a part of the action. He had opened his mouth to protest and then thought better of it. Instead, he began trying to keep up with Othniel's huge strides as not to be left behind. Although, in the long run, he may have wished he had stayed with the camels.

By the time Massoud had decided to make his grand entrance, Melchior had already reached the opening of Barak's tent. So, instead of giving Barak's firstborn a 'proper' greeting, the aged scholar simply passed Massoud as if he weren't there. A familiar anger began to boil within Massoud's heart, an odd mixture of embarrassment and pure hatred. Sayed smiled to himself, thinking that Melchior had detected far more about Massoud's true feelings than his hard hearted brother had ever meant to convey. After catching his breath,

Massoud gave Sayed a steely glance, and said through clenched teeth, "Soon, that old man will pay his proper respects to me as he has to my father for so many years. And I *do* mean *pay!*"

With that, Massoud stomped off into the tent, following the "old man," and still mumbling about the way Melchior had just treated him. Sayed followed behind Massoud into his father's presence, where his father was finishing proper negotiations with his visitors.

Inside Barak's tent, there were a number of people, all listening intently to the words of the elder patriarch. Barak was reclining upon a multitude of pillows, half sitting up and half lying down. His face, although scarred and streaked by wrinkles, still showed a great deal of strength. His eyes were intense and fixed upon those he was addressing. His hair was solid white from the top of his head to the tip of his beard. And his skin still showed the tanned nature of the herdsman, although the elder had not worked in the sun for some time.

One look at the visitors and Melchior understood why they had looked so familiar before. There were three men dressed in similar herding-type garb, only of nicer fabrics and more ceremonious. It was obvious by their dress that they respected Barak a great deal. These men were representatives of a clan of wanderers who had traveled all the way from Israel in search of a place to call their home. Their homeland was in the strong grip of the Roman government, and it was said they couldn't abide the pagan influence or the stiff taxes any longer in good conscience. Melchior had never met them, but Barak had spoken freely of them many times. It seems they had followed the caravan routes down the Arabian Peninsula, never finding any peace. That is, until they came to rest along the hill country and Barak welcomed them like brothers.

The oldest of the three visitors had just placed several gifts before Barak and said in a low reverent tone, "These gifts we bring in honor of your steadfast kindness to our people. We came from a land far away and found no place to rest our heads. But, here, at last, we have found those we can truly call family. You name your

34

ancestry back through Moses. We claim a lineage through the same bloodline through our forefather Levi. Therefore, we pledge to you and your peoples a respect and loyalty owed to blood kin. May the Lord God of both our forefathers look down upon us and bless both our peoples. Amen."

With this, all the people repeated, "Amen." All, that is, except Massoud who continued to frown, even more intensely than before. The elder who had placed the gifts stepped back behind the others, revealing to Melchior a jeweled ephod that marked the man as a priest. As far as that goes, the whole clan was made up of priests. They were a family of priests. Melchior couldn't help but wonder if, possibly, someone among these wanderers might be able to clarify the enigma of this morning's dream, and maybe, be able to verify his own interpretation concerning the star.

Melchior's thoughts were interrupted by the sound of his dear friend's voice. Barak had gathered his strength and said in a weak, but sure, voice, "I pledge our people's allegiance to your continued loyalty. As long as my people dwell along these hills, you will have your portion within it. In fact, from this day forward, your people will dwell from the Wadi-Naklah in the north to the Gabal Musa to the south."

The words had barely left Barak's lips when the anger exploded onto Massoud's face. Sayed was sure his brother was about to disrupt this sacred moment and defy their father face to face. But, fortunately, Massoud still felt a good bit of fear intermingled with partial reverence concerning his father. Instead, like a pouting child, Massoud turned and left in a silent huff. Still, although no words were spoken, his departure gained the attention of the youngest visitors, and Massoud's feelings were made quite clear.

Chapter Eight

✦ ✚ ✦

The mother's cries could be heard almost as far as Barak's tent. The pain of labor was apparently reaching its peak. Yet the cries were not as much those of birth as they were of the agony of pain. Stephanus had not been able to give much thought to the situation before him, but the closer he and Othniel got to the cries, the more apprehensive he became. Othniel had a face set with determination. His beloved master had entrusted him with a mission of great importance and there was no way he was about to let him down. He had assisted during numerous births and witnessed the wondrous miracle unfold before his very eyes many times, and all at the loving hands of his mentor, Melchior. Now, after all these years, he was on his own.

They arrived at the tent in a half run. Stephanus was grateful for the chance to catch his breath, but Othniel, unaffected, went about the task set before him. The guard at the tent entrance looked a bit concerned seeing Othniel running toward him. But as soon as the situation was explained, the guard ushered them both inside.

It was considerably darker inside the tent -- so much so that they had lamps burning on several stands. As Stephanus stepped in behind Othniel, he noticed the mother-to-be immediately. Yet, instead of the painful cries, or the size of her child-laden body, Stephanus noticed something more, something deeper. First of all, the mother was his age, and not at all what he expected. He had figured someone married to one of Melchior's friends would be very ancient. And her face, although twisted in pain, revealed a hint of incredible beauty. Her hair, although drenched with sweat, was, to Stephanus, dark, lovely strands expected from one of royal descent, not of some herdsman's wife. Her voice, although raised in a pain-stricken cry, was soft and fragile. Stephanus stood in awe for several minutes while Othniel asked the mother and her attendant questions to assess the situation.

After a moment of deep thought, Othniel turned to Stephanus and said, "You are going to have to help me!"

At first, this statement did not register at all, as Stephanus continued to contemplate the beauty of the expectant mother. Then, Othniel repeated the statement and then again. Finally, nearly fed up with getting no response, "Are you listening, boy?"

After this, Stephanus began to come around. Automatically, he stepped over to the side of Othniel, who was crouched before the mother to witness the progress of the coming child. It was then that Stephanus realized he was involved in a natural act he had never been a part of before. And then, Othniel added, "My hands are too big! You are going to have to turn the child." Then, Stephanus, considering all he had been through, began to wonder what he could have possibly done that had angered the gods so.

Barak had continued on, totally unaware of Massoud's disagreeable display. There were more words of blessing and even more of promise, and then the elder said, "You have come a long way. Johan'an, your daughter's progress is being attended to and it could possibly be awhile before we hear word concerning the child.

Please allow me to show you proper hospitality by sharing my most gracious accommodations with you and your men."

The second oldest of this trio (Johan'an, Melchior assumed) reacted without surprise, but with utter humility. "We accept your most honorable offering and would be delighted to rest here temporarily."

With that, Barak signaled Sayed to show them to a luxurious tent and assign people to see to their every need. It was obvious to Melchior that Barak respected these wanderers a great deal. As the three visitors passed the aged scholar, Melchior gave the priest and his companions a respectful bow. They each returned with a nod of their own. Melchior then began to turn his attention back to his old friend.

As the three visitors began to leave the tent, the elder priest turned to the youngest and said, "Micaiah, please stay alongside Barak. Hear the words of the magus and report to me if his condition changes."

Micaiah returned a respectful bow, and said, "As you have said, Azariah, so shall I do."

Barak had been silent for a good while, and then Melchior stepped closer and stopped, half in reverence and half in sadness. It was then that Barak noticed the frail form of his lifelong friend, and said with a bit of excitement in his voice, "Melchior, my friend, you've come at last. I was so afraid I would never see you again."

Once again, the tears returned to Melchior's wrinkled face. Then, as if to break eye contact, the scholar turned to a basin of fresh water at Barak's bedside. The act of washing was not only basic Hebrew tradition, but very necessary. As Melchior washed his hands and face, he felt the touch of a wet cloth on his feet. He looked down expecting to see one of Barak's servants. Instead, the aged patriarch himself had gotten up from his death bed to show his closest friend a final act of respect and honor.

Melchior reached down and helped his ailing friend back to his bed. There were no words either could voice to describe the emotion they felt at that moment. But, words seemed unnecessary, for each understood the other all too well. There was a time of embrace that Melchior was rather unwilling to break, possibly afraid to let go of Barak, afraid of losing him for good. But this was to be expected, as they had spent not just years, but decades pondering the ways of God together. Melchior had been there when Barak's first wife had died, and Barak gave Melchior's younger sister a burial place amongst his forefathers when she passed away. They may have not been directly blood kin, but they were brothers.

After the two elders spent a great deal of time in silent adoration, Melchior began to recall the morning's events and the good news he had brought with him. Suddenly, Melchior was filled with a feverish excitement. So much so that the magus found it hard to bring to words the news he knew his comrade must hear. After a few seconds of calming himself, Melchior grabbed his friend by the arms and, yet, could barely manage to stammer, "The star!"

Barak had known Melchior long enough to realize that his news concerning this 'star' must be extremely important and began to reply, "A star? What star?"

Melchior collected himself and took a deep breath, "The Messiah's star!"

Barak's eyes widened as he found himself speechless in the presence of such news. He began to look around and repeat, "The Messiah's star," over and over again, as if he were searching his brain for information concerning the subject. He stopped immediately, and then returned a puzzled gaze to his friend and said, "Are you sure, Melchior?"

Melchior replied with a smile and a nod as he began to laugh uncontrollably. Barak returned the smile and found himself caught up in his old friend's mirth. The two of them began to laugh and cry at the same time and continued on for some time, until they both collapsed from exhaustion into each other's embrace. After a short rest, Melchior found his breath and began to address Barak again, "There is no mistake, Barak. This star was a herald star, meaning the

Messiah is not yet born. If my calculations are correct, the star will appear twice again to us. Upon the next appearance, the Messiah will come into the world. According to ancient tradition, this star conjuncture appeared at the birth of the Deliverer, Moses, and never since with such power. And, now, for it to happen again with such incredible prominence and appearing within the constellation Pisces - Israel's sign." Melchior's excitement and volume began to grow with each word. Then his voice trailed off, "There is no other conclusion to be reached. Barak, our savior's birth is at hand."

Barak seemed in shock for a moment, and then, very seriously, he asked, "Can you tell where he is to be born?"

Melchior gave an anxious look, and replied, "All I can ascertain is that all will come to pass somewhere in Palestine, nothing more is suggested."

Barak then looked his friend eye to eye and asked, "How long do we have before the next appearance of the star?"

Melchior stopped again and began to calculate, with wrinkled brow, "I believe about three to four months."

There was another moment of silent pondering. Then, Barak gave Melchior that matter-of-fact look, and said, "Then, you must go."

Melchior returned an uneasy glance and tried to voice a protest, but could only try and avoid his friend's expectant eyes. Several times he attempted to give some excuse as to why he could never return to Israel and yet every time he opened his mouth, he returned only silence. Barak must have realized his friend was a bit unwilling, as the excitement that had at once seized Melchior now possessed the elder patriarch. He grabbed Melchior's clothes and pulled him close. Barak, then overcome with the moment, began to insist, "You *must* go! The star was sent for you to see, and our God has given you the time to make the trip. You absolutely must go to our Messiah's side!"

Barak's voice had gone from a near whisper to an angry yell. The elder was shaking all over, and yet refused to release Melchior from his iron grip. In fact, he now pulled his reluctant friend so close to him that Melchior could not escape the unwavering eyes of the dying patriarch. The look Barak gave him had turned a bit cold and angry. Barak was now crying uncontrollably, and by the look of things, he was trying his best not to strike Melchior. All those witnessing this scuffle between these aged men had no idea what to do. Sayed had returned from his father's errand, and yet even he dared not get between the two combatants. Melchior looked a bit shocked at his friend's outburst, as Barak began to speak again, a bit calmer, "Melchior, my beloved friend. I will never live to see my Messiah's face. That is why *you* must go! Do you realize that this good news may have been given to you alone? The thought must have occurred to you! You may be the only voice entrusted to herald the anointed one's coming. Therefore, you simply *must* go to his side!" Melchior tried to avoid Barak's eyes, and yet found it impossible to look away. Barak tightened his grip and reiterated, "You *must* go!" And then, after a moment of no reply, Barak pulled the wise one's face close to his own and said, "Promise me!"

This was the final straw. Melchior found himself, as usual, unable to refuse his old friend, and yet to promise a trip to the promised land? How could he possibly make the trip across desert or even over the Red Sea? His health was not much better than that of his ailing friend, and yet he did see the star. And, there was no way to tell if any other had received the star's message.

Then, suddenly, Barak began to loosen his grip. As he returned to the rest of his pillows, he whispered in Melchior's ear, "Promise me."

Immediately, all present began to draw closer, expecting the worst. Sayed appeared suddenly at his father's side, caressing the hand that had held him since childhood. Wiping the wet brow of the ancient patriarch, Sayed held back his sorrow and asked, "Father! Father! Can you hear me?"

To everyone's pleasure, Barak responded with a nod and a smile. Sayed, overcome with gratitude, buried his face upon his father's chest and prayed. Melchior had been so wrapped up with his own fear that he had forgotten his old friend's condition. And now, all he could think of was his friend dying, and him unwilling to carry out his deathbed plea. Micaiah had come to Barak's bedside also, out of fear that the elder would pass away, when suddenly someone made his way through those surrounding Barak, nearly knocking them over in the process.

"I came as fast as I could! Is he…?" Massoud began, and then stopped in horror, thinking his father had passed on. Then, seeing that his father still lived, the elder son gave a relieved, "Phew!"

Massoud's concern was obvious to all, as well as his motives. It seemed the closer Barak came to passing, the more anxious his oldest son was to collect. Melchior's anger began to swell in the presence of such greed. "Like vultures gathering, awaiting their reward!" he thought.

Then, as Melchior turned his concern back to his old friend, a familiar voice could be heard coming from outside Barak's tent. Suddenly, the magus bolted to his feet and said, "Othniel! The child!"

CHAPTER NINE

◆ ✚ ◆

I mmediately, all that were present thought the worst. Melchior himself was frozen in fear thinking to himself one death today would be too many, much less two, or possibly three. All eyes were turned toward the entrance, expectantly. Even Massoud had stopped, breathlessly anticipating the news. All ears could still hear the voice of Othniel getting closer, but still not much clearer. All hearts had stopped. All voices silenced. Then, the hulking form of Othniel appeared in the entranceway.

In his large hands he carried a bundle, which he automatically lifted up so all could see. "Barak has a son!"

Without hesitation, those who were previously frozen in fear let out a cry of joyful celebration. And Othniel, his face covered by an extensive smile, began to wade through the joyous crowd amongst shouts of praise and cries of joy. The child was passed on to Sayed, who welcomed his new brother with a smile, a shout and an elated dance. Micaiah had forgotten himself in the midst of the celebration, but soon remembered his father, Johan'an, and the orders of the priest, Azariah. Considering this, the young Hebrew turned and bolted through the entrance to pass on the glorious news.

In the midst of the shouts, Massoud began to face one of his worst nightmares. The child had not only survived, but it was a boy. Therefore, he and Sayed would be expected to share *their* inheritance with this Hebrew. Now, not only did these wandering vagabonds have the promises of the Patriarch himself, they had blood rights to this land, too. Massoud's anger began to swell again at the thought of what evil his father had brought upon his own people by not only welcoming the wanderers onto land they had no right to, but by siring a child that linked the two tribes forever. Certainly, something had to be done to stop all this, but not here, and not now.

Stephanus had been left with strict orders to monitor the mother's condition and report any changes immediately. This drew no argument from him, as it seems he had become quite taken with the young girl and knew of no better place in this entire forsaken desert he would rather have been. He remembered successfully turning the child, and then stepping back and letting Othniel finish the work. The details of what happened next were a bit sketchy. All he could remember was the cry of the child, and the silence of the mother. Come to find out, the mother had passed out from exhaustion as soon as she knew the child was alive. He remembered thinking to himself how courageous the young girl was to put the child's life before her pain. Although the mother survived, her vital signs were low and weak.

Her breath was shallow and her brow was hot and wet. Although Othniel had become quite concerned with her condition, he also knew the urgency of getting the child into the father's presence as soon as possible. Thus, Stephanus was left applying a cool cloth to the young girl's forehead and wondering whether she would live.

Suddenly, Stephanus realized this was the first time today he had taken the time to worry about someone other than himself. He had been rather rude to Melchior and Othniel earlier, and all because he hadn't taken time to realize how important this trip was to them. "I should be grateful to be alive and not…," he caught himself mid-thought. Suddenly, the tragedy of the day came crashing back down upon him: finding his father dead at the hands of Bassam and his cut-throats; the chase through the streets of Muza; the confrontation between Bassam and Melchior; the trip across the wasteland; and now the glorious birth of a new son to a dying herdsman king. It had all been enough to make Stephanus' head spin. He hadn't taken the time to grieve over his beloved father. He had been too busy running for his own life. It was then he realized that he was truly alone.

Stephanus had slipped deep into thought. So deep he didn't realize he had begun to cry uncontrollably. His tears flowed like great rivers and began to rain steadily upon the face and chest of the young mother. He continued this way for quite awhile, until a still, small voice woke him from his grief. He didn't understand the language, but the voice belonged to the young girl he had been caring for.

The young mother had survived!

The celebration in Barak's tent had reached a feverish pitch. Micaiah had returned with his father and the elder priest Azariah, who was even now kneeling in fervent prayer. Johan'an had just been handed his new grandson when the elder priest rose from his thanksgiving to give young Micaiah a new set of orders. It seemed to Micaiah the priest was always present with fresh orders.

"Boy, there has been no word given concerning your sister, Cala. Go immediately and check to see how she fared in childbirth. And report quickly. Now, go!"

With that the young boy was off like a shot. Although he would have rather stayed and celebrated with the men, he knew not to question Azariah.

After a moment of adoration, Johan'an turned and began to move in toward Barak. The frenzied group quieted to a whisper. Suddenly, every step the proud grandfather took could be heard throughout the tent. Johan'an was almost half the age of the ailing patriarch, and his daughter, Barak's bride, was half that. But the marriage, although arranged, became a joy for all concerned. Barak and Cala made an odd looking couple, but their love and adoration for each other, and for their respected tribes, grew each day. The announcement of the young bride's pregnancy pleased most all who heard. And, now, the culmination of a romance, not just between two people, but two peoples, had been realized.

Barak reached out to take the child with once-strong hands that now had to receive help caressing the newborn. Once sure, Johan'an stepped away as Barak held the baby close to his bosom and cried tears of anticipated joy. Most could hear him singing under his breath in an old Aramaic dialect, a thanksgiving written by his ancestors long ago. Half way through, Azariah joined him, recognizing the ageless Psalm. Then, Melchior chimed in, to complete the majestic chorus of the ancient patriarchs. Once finished, all three now in tears, Barak gathered his courage as well as his breath and began, "Azariah, Melchior, and me share memories of being forced from the Promised Land, if not first hand, through the stories told by the elders by campfire. We live in exile today, but there is a day coming, my children, when our peoples will stand on the shore of the Jordan and worship on Zion's holy mount again. And now, I feel certain that time is drawing nearer."

The ailing frame of the respected elder seemed to gain an inner strength. His eyes focused upon those present around him and his voice took on certain urgency, as if this was to be the last message given to his people. Holding the child close to his heart, he continued, "This is to be a glorious day for all our people -- the birth of a new son I feel shall be a blessing to us all. Please do not grieve at my passing. My time upon this earth has been long and blessed. The future belongs to the young, and there it shall remain.

This now brings me to the passing of one generation to another, the gift of my blessing."

At this one word, Massoud's heart leaped as if from his chest. He had already poised himself, ready to accept the mantle of leadership rightfully his, and yet he still tried not to over-play the moment.

Barak stopped in mid-thought and gave Melchior a look as if something between the two held his mind in check for the moment. And, then, a smile and an assured nod seemed to settle the whole question. Melchior, however, wasn't quite sure what the question, or the answer, had been. Barak turned his attention upon the child he held in his caress and gave another smile and an even more assured nod, then continued, "It has been brought to my attention that in the early morning sky a special star made its first of several appointed appearances. My learned friend, Melchior, assures me this holy star was sent to herald the coming birth of the anticipated Holy One of Israel; the coming of the Messiah; the Savior of us all."

The beloved patriarch found himself overcome with joy as his ancient tears began to track the many lines that covered his ancient face. Melchior shared this moment with his friend, convinced that all he had read in the stars was true. Yet, Azariah, steeped in the old Hebrew Levitical codes, thought to himself, "How could anything as holy as the promised Messiah be involved with star gazing or sooth saying?" Indeed, he feared that Barak had made a grave mistake befriending the magus after all.

Barak continued, "For most of my long life, I have cried to the Most High God for some sign concerning the promised Savior. Unfortunately, up to this time, all I could see was the world's darkness overcoming Israel's faint, failing light. Yet, I held an inner hope that someday my God would answer me."

The tears began to flow as Barak's joy could no longer be withheld. Decades of pent up emotion rushed from the elder's weary eyes. Yet, his frail body didn't fail him. Instead, he seemed to gain courage and strength with every word. At times he could be heard whispering a prayer, or a Psalm, or some sort of thanksgiving under his breath. Between thoughts, it was as if he were gaining strength from heaven itself, or possibly heaven had begun to direct his every word. Whatever was happening, all present knew that what Barak was about to say was of the utmost importance.

Barak then took a deep, cleansing breath and looked down into the face of the blessed newborn. A smile broke out across his ancient face once more as he went on, "And, now, I hold in my arms proof that my God hears. I asked for one last son to complete my joy and he has granted me this. I have pleaded for God's promised Messiah to come and he has heard my cry. Therefore, my son, you shall be called Samuel, for my God hears my voice and remembers his promise. Just as the prophet Samuel was born to Hannah in her old age, my Samuel is born unto me in my last days. Just as Hannah's Samuel was born special for holy service, my Samuel is born this day under the holy star of the Messiah. And, therefore, this little child is set apart for a most holy calling."

Barak stopped and gave all around him an intense look and then proclaimed, "Let it be written this day that Barak, blessed of God and honored by men, appoints his most holy blessing along with the honored mantle of leadership according to the appointment of God and not the tradition of men..."

The elder, now visibly weakened, had lain back, resting on his bed, still holding young Samuel close to his heart. His breath had become shallow, his eyes weakened. Yet, his embrace of the child would not be broken. Massoud had knelt beside Barak in anticipation of his anointing as his father's heir. Sayed could hardly restrain himself, his grief nearly overcoming him. It was obvious to all that Barak was breathing his last breath upon this earth, and upon his last words the fate of his people would rest. The dying patriarch motioned for a servant to bring the anointing oil and asked Sayed privately to bring another container. Another servant had been at his bed side, unseen until now, recording every word Barak uttered. When all was in place, the elder finished with these words, "This day is to be a day of celebration, considering the good news I bring you this day. Our Messiah's star is seen and his birth imminent. Melchior, my most honored of friends, I give to you a most precious gift. Here within this flask is a most valuable ointment, the precious fragrance of myrrh intended to be administered to me upon my burial. It is the most expensive thing I have. Take it and present it to the Messiah upon his birth in my place, seeing as I will never see the Holy One's face myself. I expect you to fulfill this one request and may God be with you upon your journey."

Othniel, now standing behind his beloved master, almost voiced his opposition, but Melchior, sensing his young friend's apprehension, put up his hand as if to stop him from speaking. The two elders were once again eye to eye, but this time Melchior didn't give any excuses, only an accepting nod as he took the flask from Sayed's hands. Barak, struggling now to speak, continued on with the task at hand. The servant then tipped the mouth of the other container onto the frail hands of Barak. As the anointing oil poured onto his hand, he gathered a last bit of strength and said, "As my father anointed me heir of all God had blessed him with, so must I anoint an heir to carry on after my passing. Therefore, considering the sign of the star and the birth of my child under the influence of this most holy appearance, I anoint Samuel my heir and appoint Sayed and Massoud, his brothers, as joint guardians of our people until such time as Samuel grows into adulthood."

With these words, Barak applied the oil to the baby's forehead and set in motion the future of his people. And then, Barak's last recorded words were, "May the Most High God of all Creation and his appointed Holy Messiah have mercy upon all our peoples. Amen."

And as the light faded from the eyes of the weary patriarch amid tears and prayers, there was a collective agreement summed up in the word, "Amen."

Chapter Ten

. + .

S tephanus found himself frozen, eye to eye with the young girl. There was a moment of terrible silence. Then the new mother reached up, wiping away the tears cascading from his smooth but broken features. Her voice rang out again, a little louder and yet infused with the same bit of elegance. It became clear to Stephanus that the problem between them wasn't the language, but the dialect.

After listening a bit more closely, with a slight bit of difficulty, Stephanus began to translate the words of the beautiful young mother.

"What is your name, sad one?" rolled once more from the lips of the exhausted mother.

Stephanus was caught speechless. The darkest recesses of his soul were left open for this stranger to peer into, and yet he was reluctant to close himself to her. Her eyes were peering in deep, and instead of thinking less of him, as was his fear, she seemed to show a bit of understanding and a profound compassion. It was as if she knew the pain he felt, and yet she couldn't really know, could she?

Finally, after a moment that seemed like an eternity, Stephanus forgot himself and his pain and turned his attention back toward his task. "How are you feeling?" he asked. He paused, realizing he didn't even know her name.

Then, the mother, apparently sensing a pause that needed filling, spoke. "Cala. My name is Cala. I feel tired and a bit weak, but I will be fine." Then she stopped and looked around, a bit of worry arising in her dark eyes, and continued, "My baby. Is my baby . . .?"

"Your son is fine. Othniel took him."

Cala broke in, finally realizing, "You are with the magus, are you not?"

Her eyes had exploded with wonder and discovery. The way she said "magus" led Stephanus to believe she was, at the very least, mystified with Melchior and his title. And this also seemed to increase her interest in Stephanus, which didn't bother him in the least. She seemed to forget everything else that was happening around her as she asked, "Are you Melchior's new apprentice?"

Stephanus wasn't very sure of the answer to that question, but clamoring for her attention, he answered, "Well, in a way I guess I am."

"What does he call you?" Cala asked.

"What does he call me?" Stephanus thought to himself, *What kind of question is that? The old man has never called me by my real name anyway, always Stephen!*

"Has he not given you a name?" she asked.

Stephanus began to wonder to himself if Melchior was indeed trying to 'rename' him after all, and, then, gave her a slightly defiant, "My name is Stephanus."

She apparently picked up on his frustration and decided to move on, "Well, Stephanus, where did Othniel take my son?"

"He took him to be presented to his father." He broke off there, seeing that anything uttered after the word "father" was not going to be heard. Stephanus had forgotten about Barak's condition and instantly saw something in her eyes he hadn't seen. . . well. . . for a long time -- compassionate love.

The compassion soon turned to concern as Cala tried to get up out of bed. "I must see my husband." With that, she began to fall and Stephanus quickly braced her.

"You really need your rest. You shouldn't try to walk."

He caught eye contact with the young mother again, and now the concern had turned to unwavering determination. Stephanus finally surrendered and said, offering Cala a hand, "At least let me assist you. You aren't strong enough to walk on your own."

Cala hesitated, and then accepted the hand of the young stranger, realizing that it may be the only way she would get to her ailing husband in time. She stood up clumsily, at times falling onto Stephanus' long frame, using him as a strong and sure crutch. As the two turned toward the outside, they faced another figure blocking the entrance. Swiping the cloth away from his face, young Micaiah ordered, "Who are you and where are you taking my sister?"

Stephanus just stood there in shock as though he had actually been caught doing something unseemly. Cala pulled herself up, giving her brother an angry eye, "This young man is with the magus and is simply helping me to my husband's bedside. Don't take that tone concerning him."

Micaiah, giving his sister a disgruntled look and Stephanus an untrusting stare, barked back, "Well, personally, I have no need for anyone associated with that magician. So, if you don't mind, I'll take my sister from here."

Micaiah practically forced Stephanus to the side, picked up his sister and carried her through the tent entrance. Stephanus' first thought was to push back, but thought better of it, fearing for Cala's safety. So he simply followed on, hearing Cala say something to her brother about how rude he had been. Her brother had replied, "By all that's holy, he has the look of the pagan about him."

Cala gave no reply, only a "Humph" of disapproval. It was apparent that Micaiah did not share his sister's enthrallment with Melchior in the least. Stephanus, losing ground behind them, began to wonder if his life would ever be returned to the degree of normalcy he experienced before his father's death. After a short consideration, he began to doubt it.

CHAPTER ELEVEN

◆ ✛ ◆

It had been almost eight days since Barak's passing and Melchior's pain seemed only to grow. He had spent the past nights in a dreamless sleep, if it could truly be called sleep. Now, he found himself once again kneeling before his friend's tomb. He had collapsed, partly in prayer and partly in surrender, to the deep depression threatening to overcome his very soul. There was just too much to remember, and most all of it was just too painful.

He was not alone in his pain. All of Barak's kin, as well as every visitor, seemed to be in a constant state of mourning. Melchior remembered the look in Sayed's eyes -- the blank, glassy stare from eyes filled with darkness and tears. It was difficult to forget this look, for it was on most of the faces Melchior had passed since. He had tried to forget the cries of Barak's young bride, Cala. Her wails made the mourning of all the others seem like whispers. The sage had never seen such an outpouring of emotion. It was truly the product of a tragic pain. It was as if she had been the elder patriarch's wife from his youth and not just for one short year. No one expected such true love and devotion from such a short life together. Yet, Cala went through the traditional mourning and separation, not so much out of a sense of obligation, but out of true love and respect.

A dark cloud had seemed to settle over the hill country, and its shadow was at its darkest over the heart of Melchior. He had never had a friend like Barak, who shared as much of his past, present, as well as his expectations of the future. They were kindred spirits in so many ways, and Melchior's life would never truly recover from this striking blow. He had never felt such loss. The past seemed meaningless, his present too painful, and his future? Well, it seemed at this point there was no seeing through the abject darkness of his pain.

But, there was more to Melchior's remorse than the loss of a friend. He had cared for these people since becoming a magus in his own right, carrying with him the office of Priest, as well as wise man. And now, their patriarch having fallen, their destiny lay somewhere between a child born under a holy star and two brothers left to care for it all. It would be years before the child would be wise enough to lead them. And his brothers were not always of the same mind. Melchior feared for their future.

Then, Melchior's memories wandered farther until once again he was looking into the eyes of Barak, making promises that seemed impossible to keep, agreeing to a quest he surely couldn't make. But those eyes . . . Barak's eyes still searched him . . . implored him . . . held him to his promises. How could he make such a trip? What did he expect to find? Was he absolutely sure about the star? Could he have been wrong?

After a moment of silence, Melchior knew all the answers to his questions, especially his assurance of the star's meaning. He was sure. He would stake everything upon it, and would probably end up having to. Yet, how could he leave Barak's kin, knowing their future was in such jeopardy? What plans did God have for this people, and, more importantly, what plans did the Almighty have for Melchior? Not meaning to question the Almighty, he instead repressed further contemplation in this direction and the pain returned. The tears flowed and the darkness overcame him.

"Though I walk through the valley of the shadow of death," a voice chimed in. Recognizing both the psalm and the voice, Melchior returned almost bitterly, "I will fear no evil, for You are with me."

The elder rose up from his prone position slowly, wearily, to look upon the image of another holy man breaking the darkness. Azariah smiled and continued, "Your rod and staff comfort me. You prepare a table before me in the presence of my enemies . . ."

The priest's voice broke off, as if disturbed by his own psalm of comfort. He offered Melchior a hand. Once up, they found a resting place among the rocks and began to share the darkness, or maybe break the darkness together.

"I felt your grief across the encampment. I was compelled to come, and yet, I am not sure what to do next." Azariah looked a bit rattled as he spoke, and truly acted as though there was nothing else in mind to say.

"You are a man driven by the spirit of God, Azariah. I have a great adoration for a man with such a gift. You are blessed among men and I am blessed simply by your presence."

Azariah bowed slightly in appreciation, and then suddenly continued, "Actually, there is more." The priest looked almost too embarrassed to go on. Maybe the very fact that he was there at all said something. The simple act of talking with a magus, much less admitting that the spirit moved him thus spoke volumes. Azariah would never have come to this point on his own accord. Therefore, Melchior knew that God must be at work here and knew better than to take this unexpected dialogue for granted.

"I have come concerning the star."

The "star." Everything seemed to revolve around its appearance. It seemed to move this sad little drama from the very beginning. And now what? The next act? Melchior had tried to put it behind him, bury it deep within the dark recesses of his beleaguered mind. But, God seemed unwilling to leave it there. And so, the light broke the darkness once again, in a way, as the elder fought to remember.

"If you have come to question the accuracy of my findings, there is no question you could possibly ask that I have not asked myself. There is no doubt in my mind and my spirit confers."

Azariah considered his words carefully to not become combative. "But astrology?! Melchior, you know the ancient scriptures -- the law. How? How can this be?"

Melchior gave his peer a weary look and went on, "Don't you mean, how can I?" With this, Azariah returned a glance, revealing his embarrassment and the wise one went on. "It is all right, Azariah. I am not offended. I have struggled with the duality of my life from early on. At the death of my father, I swore never to leave his ways. Not many years after, I lost the rest of my family to Bedouin bandits. My Uncle had taken me in... I was still young -- about Stephen's age."

"If not for the kindness of a traveling stranger, I would have died there in the desert. But my life, instead of being over, had just begun. My benefactor was revealed to be an exiled Babylonian magus who took me in and taught me his knowledge. Neither my faith, nor my knowledge of the stars, has ever failed me. The astronomical readings I take are as real to me as the scripture I hold dear. I can't ask you to understand, Azariah. But the stars didn't lie and my heart knows all this to be true."

Azariah, still visibly burdened, continued on, "So. What next? What do the stars say now?"

Melchior bowed his head, "I do not know. I haven't been able to get a clear reading since . . . the star."

The old man turned away from Azariah and toward the tomb of his departed friend. "All I see is darkness . . . overcoming . . . mind-numbing darkness." A tear broke the solemn features of the once hopeful man. The pain returned.

Sayed really believed he was prepared for his father's passing. He really thought the months of seeing his father fall steadily under the powerful force of death would ready him for these dark days. He was absolutely sure he could let his father go on to be with his ancestors without the troublesome ritual of mourning. Sayed really thought he could bury his father without a tear.

He was wrong on all accounts.

Absolutely nothing could have prepared him for the shock of his father's death. He had lost his mother when he was much younger and never really remembered anything about her or her death. This was the first experience he actually had with the death of one so close, and it wasn't turning out to be a pleasant one.

He had been spending most of his days in solitude, alone in his tent. When he had ventured out, it was usually at night and he usually found some dark corner in which to hide. He would listen to the conversations of the watchmen as they warmed themselves by the fire. Most of what they said was idle chatter, but after a few days, the talk became frightening.

By the seventh night after Barak's passing, the talk seemed to turn ugly. While sulking in the shadows, as had become his habit, Sayed overheard a group of herdsmen talking with the watchmen around the campfire.

"Come now, Abishur, surely you won't stand there and defend those Hebrews!" The man speaking was Falah, one of the more powerful clan leaders amongst the herdsmen ranks. "After muscling their way onto our lands, which is bad enough, they worked their way into our great departed leader's bed. And they used the affections of that young wench to soften Barak's heart and mind for their ultimate goal -- total control of not only our land, but our people as well!"

"Falah! How soon you forget that it was the will of Barak for those people to move onto that land and for him to marry young Cala. You make our great fallen leader sound like a mindless fool!" Abishur had risen from his seat and had begun to shout.

Falah lowered his voice and motioned while he talked, as if to calm Abishur down. After all, Abishur was almost a foot taller and wider than the herdsman.

"We all loved and respected Barak with a boundless devotion. But, how many great men have been known to be taken in by the charms of a younger woman, only to be used unwillingly? All I'm saying is, he was used."

A younger, smaller member of the group then spoke up. "If I may be so bold? My family has served Barak these last few years and, concerning your opinions, nothing could be further from the truth."

Falah was now the one showing his anger as he stood and pointed at the young boy. "Are you calling me a liar?"

"Oh, no, Falah!" The young boy, whose name was Taymen, was visibly shaken, but not from his opinion. "I only say that Cala and her people have been nothing less than loyal to the will and whim of Barak from the beginning. Loyal!"

"Taymen! Taymen, my dear boy. Suffice it to say that, as honorable as your statement is, you are still but a boy and have not even known a woman yet. You could not know the treachery that exists within such a relationship, for you have yet to know or understand women at all. When one falls for such a woman, he is blind to her ways." Falah paused, grinning from ear to ear, "Perhaps you are smitten by her too?"

The whole group erupted into laughter, yelling, mocking, and jeering at young Taymen, who then disappeared into the crowd in embarrassment. After the group calmed down, Abishur continued, "I still tend to agree with the young boy. I have seen nothing from these people to suggest treachery. They show nothing but love and loyalty toward Barak, even after his passing."

"Abishur! You're as blind as the young boy! Or are you also taken with their women?" Falah laughed, but only a few joined him. For all who were there knew Abishur was a recent widower himself. And by the look on his face, he didn't consider Falah's comment the least bit amusing.

Abishur, ready to pounce on the smaller Falah, then felt a hand on his shoulder. All those around the fire stopped where they were. The anticipated fight would have to be postponed. As the two combatants backed off, Sayed broke the frigid silence. "Has it been so long? Were the words of my father lost to you all? Barak was a man of integrity and not one to be taken 'unwittingly' by anyone!"

Sayed had everyone's attention now. There were even those who had been shaken from their sleep by his outburst who were now poking their heads out of their tents just enough to see what the commotion was. Seeing none of the group was about to argue with him, Sayed continued, "We may consider ourselves more Midianite than Hebrew, but our blood was joined long before my father's marriage to young Cala. We are of the same lineage, same traditions, same God! That same God brought our peoples together after years of separation. And, now, who among you is about to let greed and jealousy come between you and God's providence?"

No one dared to answer. All present, even those who disagreed with Sayed, respected him almost as much as they did his father. And not one of them was about to embarrass his clan to prove a point. Sayed gave them all an extremely angry look, his chest heaving. He knew to continue would be fruitless. They would neither challenge him, nor change their poisoned minds. Sayed turned away, as not to embarrass himself by going on. It was obvious to him that the problem wasn't those arguing around the file, but the poison's source. Stomping off in an almost steady march, young Sayed decided to head this off before it got any worse. He knew that, if you want to kill a snake, you don't cut off its tail. You cut it off at the head.

Chapter Twelve

◆ **✚** ◆

S ayed had tried to stay rational, as he had so many other times before in confrontations with his older brother. The problem was always that Massoud thrived on argument and strife, while Sayed had always tried to be the healing voice amidst the storm. There had also been their father to take into consideration -- a little matter of respect. But, that too was something his brother had had a problem with since early on. Sayed had kept a tight lip for far too long. He had put up with his brother's dishonorable ranting regarding their father. Yes, Sayed had really tried to stay rational, but he now found himself unable to contain himself.

Sayed had practically marched the breadth of the encampment to find Massoud, and had taken most of the dark morning doing it. He wasn't in his tent, and he wasn't in the usual places where Massoud could be found. Finally, a bit tired, Sayed looked in the last place he expected to find his missing brother. And needless to say, that is exactly where he found him. For who would have guessed that his malicious brother would be found, only about eight days of his father's passing, bedding down in his father's tent.

This move alone proved his intentions clearly. It was all Sayed could do to keep from taking a club to his bother as it was. And to make matters worse, Massoud was not alone. It really wouldn't have made matters any better if he had brought his wife of seven years with him to make his move into his father's tent. But Massoud really completed his disgraceful dishonoring of their father by bedding some young wench on the very bed which their father had died not eight days before.

Massoud saw his younger brother come in and gave him that matter-of-fact kind of look. He didn't seem at all surprised. On the contrary, he had that look on his face as if he'd planned the whole thing and expected Sayed to be here at this exact moment. Massoud smiled and whispered something into the young girl's ear. After which, she laughed, pulled a tunic over her once innocent body, and passed Sayed with a sheepish grin across her face as she exited into the night.

As usual, it was Massoud who spoke first. "Come in, my brother. I have been expecting you." He watched Sayed closely, almost hungrily; much like a wild animal would stalk his prey. As Sayed made his way into his brother's presence, he could find no words adequate to express his rage. His anger welled up inside like a volcano, threatening eruption, but not carrying it out. Not yet.

All Sayed could manage was, "What are you doing here?"

Massoud didn't even flinch, but answered with a quick and steady strike, "I am merely taking my rightful place -- the place where I was born to sit. As the oldest, I lead the next generation. That is the way it has always been. That is the way it will always be."

With that, Massoud sat back, like his word was to be final in the matter. And, most of the time, in days past, that would have been the end of that. But not tonight. The whole experience of his father's death came crashing down upon Sayed all over again. It had changed him a great deal. And, today, Sayed would not let it go at that.

Melchior had experienced a great deal of darkness during his long life, but never had he known such overpowering blackness as even now threatened his soul. The elder had once again begun to slip into that deep, mesmerizing dream state, where he would try without success to shake the pain that ate at him from within. As the sorrow and loss began to overtake him, a hand firmly gripped his shoulder, serving as an anchor to reality. Melchior, tired and emotionally spent, turned to face the elder priest. He was now eye to eye with a man who understood his emotional state more than any man living.

Azariah proved unwilling to let Melchior give in that easily. For, no matter what differences the two had, their past and their futures were destined to be intertwined. For a long moment, neither could find the words to communicate their feelings. Then, Azariah reached deep inside and spoke without restraint, almost inspired, "Barak was lucky to have a friend like you. It is obvious that you loved him with a love that transcends that of a brother. Your sorrow honors our friend. But, Melchior, it was Barak's life that ended here, not yours."

Azariah had Melchior's attention now. The magus gave the priest a look that made him glad. Melchior was a rational man. For if the magus had been prone to physical outbursts, Azariah would have been in for the fight of his life. Instead, Melchior just turned away, trying hard to avoid the priest's prying eyes. But it was of no use. Melchior, even now facing away from Azariah, still felt the eyes of the priest searching him, looking into his heart.

"Barak had done that . . . many times," he thought.

"You are an aged man, Melchior. But God is not finished with you, yet," Azariah said with assurance.

Melchior turned again, that sad emptiness still in his eyes, and said, "How can you know that for sure? How can we know that God is not finished with His work in me yet? I have accomplished much in my life, priest. I am fully prepared to meet the Most High today if need be. In fact, I would welcome death with open arms."

Melchior stopped and looked off into the distance, as if waiting for God's own chariot to come pick him up. Then, he continued,

"This world's darkness is no longer bearable for me to continue my work. Barak was one of the last great men of light. And now, that light is out. Without his leadership, there may be no light in the future for any of us. I just do not see any reason to fight on."

With that, Melchior turned once again to the priest, as if waiting for an answer. There was dread silence as morning broke across the hill country. Unfortunately, from where the two of them were sitting, only shadows prevailed. And, then, suddenly, a ray of marvelous, morning light broke over the tomb area. As if in sync with the glorious sun, Azariah looked deep into the eyes of the troubled magus and answered, "What about the star?"

Chapter Thirteen

◆ ✝ ◆

Micaiah had chosen to stay with his sister, Cala, during the last week as she refused to return to Barak's tent until the proper time of separation and mourning passed. He had never known his sister to be so ritualistic, but she felt strongly that this was the greatest way to honor her departed husband. And, anyway, it seemed that she had taken the time to work through a great deal of the pain and loss, and was coming out, in the end, better for it.

Young Samuel had shown himself to be a strong child with an athlete's health. Cala gave praise continually for this fact, and also for the fact that both their lives had been spared. She would miss Barak, but would see him every day in the eyes of Samuel. That her son had been given Barak's blessing overwhelmed her. She found herself both pleased and troubled at this fact. Cala wasn't certain what the future held for them, but she knew it was all in the hands of the Almighty.

Micaiah continued to be concerned about the attention the stargazer's servant, Stephanus, was giving his sister. It was an outright disgrace the way he fawned over her. For, although she allowed no others into her presence, the young pagan found every reason possible to show up at her tent's entrance; a bucket of water; a bit of food; medicinal herbs or holy incense. It didn't seem to matter what it was, it always seemed to be delivered by that conjurer's apprentice. And unfortunately, although he had tried repeatedly, he seemed unable to deter Stephanus throughout the day.

What really annoyed Micaiah was that all this didn't seem to bother Cala at all. In fact, she seemed to brighten up when she knew Stephanus had been by. She tried to hide it, but her older brother knew her better. And, to really make matters worse, the boy had been nothing less than kind to him since they met. Micaiah wished the pagan would do something that could warrant the anger he felt, but he never did. This gave Micaiah a guilty feeling he really didn't like.

Micaiah remembered wondering whether he and Stephanus would meet again this morning as he went out to greet the day. Later, he would wish he had met up with the pagan rather than experiencing what came next. He had just stepped out of the tent when he noticed etchings in the dirt spanning the entrance of the tent. He knelt down to look it over and realized the signs and symbols were totally foreign to him. Yet, he could make out enough to know he didn't like it one bit. And so, as Cala slept on (she had had a long night with Samuel), Micaiah ran and brought back Johan'an.

What happened next haunted Micaiah the rest of his life. Johan'an knelt as Micaiah had done and began to attempt to decipher the markings. Yet, unlike his son, the father seemed to know exactly what they meant. Johan'an simply stood, staring off into the distance, and shed a single tear. Wiping it away, he turned to Micaiah and said, "Stay with Cala! I will take care of this myself!"

"The star . . ."

Melchior was frozen in his tracks. He had rushed across the wasteland to bring Barak the 'Good News', and now it seemed he wanted to do nothing more than forget he had ever seen the astral messenger. It was clear. Unfortunately, Melchior's mind wasn't. For the first time in his life, the old one's thoughts were a muddle of light and darkness. The wise man that people all over Arabia came to for advice was lost without hope.

Or so Melchior thought.

Azariah spoke on, gaining boldness with every word. It really seemed odd, hearing Azariah pleading the star's case, but the priest was a holy man of the Most High God of Israel and a mouthpiece of the Almighty. On the surface, Azariah may have questioned Melchior's means, but deep down in the spirit of the priest, the spirit of God stirred. And the Spirit of God knew what had to be done.

"Not much more than a week ago, you knelt by Barak's death bed and claimed to have seen the Messiah's star. And now, here you are, huddled by his tomb, full of fear and sorrow. You claim the Messiah is to be born in Judea soon, yet you refuse to rush to his side! What happened, Melchior? Has the faith you rode in here on died and been buried with Barak?"

Melchior looked dazed as he attempted feebly to answer, "Well . . . I . . ."

But, before he could put a sentence together, Azariah blasted, "Do you really believe what you say you saw in the stars?"

"I know what I saw," Melchior returned, with his head bowed.

"Do you really believe the star to be a sign of the Messiah's coming?"

"The message is clear." Melchior looked up, pain overcoming his aged face.

"What purpose would God have had in sending the 'messenger' to you and not to the Holy Priests of Israel?"

"I have never thought of that," Melchior replied, not sure where this was going.

"If you believe God has made his announcement through the stars, you must realize that those who keep both temple and synagogue in Israel weren't watching." Azariah slowed a bit and finished, "They weren't watching!"

It all rushed back to Melchior. The first sight of the star and the search through the scrolls of Holy Scripture; the words he had spoken to Barak; the promise. And then reality set in. He felt his age creep up on him, the death itself hunting him, haunting him. And for the first time in his long, aged life, Melchior became honest with, not only himself, but the Levitical Priest, Azariah.

"I'm not really here out of grief and loss, am I?" Melchior asked, trying to understand the darkest secret in his dark world: himself, "I am not afraid to leave my friend Barak's tomb as much as I fear the journey to my own."

There was a long silence between them and then Melchior concluded, "I am afraid to die!"

Azariah found himself again and joined in, "How can one such as you fear death? You believe in the Most High, do you not?"

Melchior gave the priest a solemn look and answered, "It is not what comes after death that scares me. It is what has come before. I am afraid that I have failed in my life-long search for truth and light. I know the Most High, but I don't KNOW the Most High!"

Melchior began to shed bitter tears as he opened his soul to the one person he thought would never see him eye to eye. "It is all very clear to me now! I cannot complete my mission in life without traveling to Judea. But I can't travel to the Promised Land without risking death along the way. And, if I die along the way, I meet my master, having failed him."

Melchior was really weeping now. It was obvious that the magus was in the most confused of states. It was also obvious that it was a most unfamiliar state. Azariah walked slowly over to the magus' side and put his hand gently onto the elder's shoulder. As the aged Melchior looked up into the priest's soft, caring eyes, both men seemed to arrive at the same place at the same time. Azariah looked deep into Melchior's tear filled eyes and said what both of them seemed to be thinking, "My dear man! Do you not understand? It is not the destination that matters as much as the journey! What matters is that you have been called, and that you, as God's servant, will answer. God only knows what will transpire along the way, but He also knows the heart of the man He has called. He wants nothing more from you than what you have to offer, Melchior. What have you to offer Him?"

They both were transfixed for a while, locked in a mutual stare. Then, Melchior's tears stopped as he stood to face Azariah. Simultaneously, the two of them smiled and embraced. Obviously, God was at work here, as two vastly different individuals showed the same moment of revelation. Azariah still wasn't sure he understood or approved of Melchior's reading of 'the star,' but at this moment, it didn't seem to matter.

The two had just released one another, looking a bit embarrassed and awkward. Then Melchior opened his mouth about to speak when, suddenly, Stephanus appeared. He had just come off a dead run and was quite winded. He had only enough strength left to look up from his bent over position and say, "Come quickly! There is trouble!"

light which was just appearing over the hill country. As if in a daze, Massoud continued to look out into the sunshine as he leaned upon a ceremonial spear that had been given to Barak by Cala's people. In an almost memorized speech, Massoud went on, "Father told me once how our people controlled a great deal of the coastline from old Ocelis to the mighty Gulf of Agaba. It can be that way again. And it starts here. We have given up too much already. I will give up no more."

Sayed was beginning to see the big picture now. Massoud had been thinking and scheming about this for some time and had decided to lead his people into a "golden age" of conquest. He had never known his brother to be quite so disillusioned before, but now it seemed he had crossed the line. What scared him the most was that his elder brother was not so much crazy as he was consumed with greed. His lust for power, feeding off some story of days of old, had gotten to the point of infatuation. And, probably, when his father gave his blessing to the young baby and didn't deliver it to the ready hands of Massoud, it simply pushed him over the edge.

Sayed was still in shock when Massoud continued, "Of the thirteen elders, seven stand behind me already. A force in Muza awaits my word. I have a strong enough force mounting to not only secure the coastline surrounding Muza, but to march upon the Hebrew encampments to the north and run them back to their "promised land." You will either stand with me, or against me. There is no middle ground here, brother. You must choose!"

The more Sayed heard, the more he couldn't believe what he was hearing. Massoud had drawn his line in the sand, and now Sayed was forced to make a grave decision. In the end, though, there was only one answer to be given. "I cannot stand with you, brother, nor can I simply allow you to disgrace our father's name or our people. I must see to it that you are stopped." Sayed had begun to walk with an angry march to the tent entrance as he added, "You will be stopped!"

As Sayed started past Massoud, he hadn't noticed his older brother strengthening his grip on the spear. Nor did he see the fire return to Massoud's eyes. Sayed had become an obstacle. Too many within the tribes still respected him. He could not be allowed to voice his opposition. This fact left Massoud no other option.

CHAPTER FIFTEEN

· ✚ ·

The etchings in the sand were getting harder and harder to read, but the message was clear. Melchior had even read it several times hoping that it would somehow read differently, but it never changed. He had seen it before; An old, mystic curse set against a newborn child with lethal intentions. Obviously, young Samuel had an enemy.

Of course, Melchior never put much stock in such Bedouin curses. But Johan'an must have taken it as more of a threat than a curse. And, Melchior was not so sure he was wrong in doing so. The elder closed his eyes in prayer, partly in an effort to postpone delivery of the morbid message, but mostly to call upon the only source of light left in his aged life.

He had finally come to grips with it all. As difficult as it was to imagine him making this trip, he was called to it, born for it. It seemed typical, though. The Enemy strikes so quickly -- never gives a man time to savor the victory -- never time to rejoice in a right deci ion made. He should have expected it, really.

"What does it say, Melchior?" Azariah spoke, addressing the magus like an old friend. It reminded Melchior of how Barak used to speak to him. Azariah could see that the old star gazer had drifted off again, and put his hand on Melchior's shoulder and said, "Is it as foreboding as it looks?"

Melchior looked up; his eyes said it all, and his voice echoed, "I am afraid so. It is a curse; wishing death upon the child in the tent."

Azariah had begun to cry, and tore the front of his garment in both anger and sorrow. The Levite didn't believe for one minute that the curse held one ounce of power. Like Melchior, he didn't put much credence in such things. But, it was the intentions behind it that sent chills down the spine. Whoever etched this particular curse revealed a burning hatred rarely seen; a prejudice that could kill. Then, the priest turned to young Micaiah and asked, "You say Johan'an went to find Massoud?"

Micaiah answered swiftly and respectfully, "Yes, Azariah. He ordered me to stay here or I could have followed him."

"Yes, son, you did the right thing as usual, both in staying with Cala and sending Stephanus after me. You could have done no better." Azariah began to pace around the front of the tent and then stopped and spoke, not even looking up, "I should have seen it all coming. The elder son, expecting to rise to a leadership role over his father's people, finds himself instead a servant of an outsider's child . . .I really should have expected all this . . ."

"How could you expect such bedevilment from a son of Barak? How could any of us have seen this?" Micaiah was standing, fists clenched and the pitch of his voice rising, "We knew Massoud was sour about your presence in the hill country from the very beginning, but *this?*"

The young Hebrew had begun to gather stares from those passing by. It was fully morning now and the camp had come alive with activity. Most had ignored them. But, there were many eyes upon them. And, most were returning indignant stares.

Azariah noticed this, where Micaiah had not, and decided to stop him from going on. "Let us take this discussion into the tent, shall we?"

But, before the priest could give his young grandson a directing touch on the arm, Micaiah reacted with hostility, "What? We have no time for idle discussions! My father is walking into that wolf, Massoud's, den and may end up being the devil's prey! We have to go now!"

Azariah had now gained a strong grip on Micaiah's arm and hissed, "Quiet down, Micaiah. Your ranting is of no use to us here, and, what is worse, you stand a good chance of upsetting your grieving sister. There is no reason to cause an incident until we know more about the situation."

Micaiah composed himself, trying to be respectful and yet he blurted, "Until we know more? What else is there to know? My nephew is receiving death threats, and Massoud is most likely involved. And besides that, my father is even now cornering that dog in his lair. My place is at his side!"

"Micaiah!" Azariah now spoke in a tone that had everyone's attention. "Whatever Massoud has on his heart to do or think is beside the point. We owe it to his father, Barak, to handle this situation respectfully. But you are right on one account at least. I have heard enough. If Johan'an handles this with the diplomacy you seem to have, there will most certainly be an incident that all involved will regret for some time."

The elder turned as if to follow after Johan'an alone, and then stopped and spoke once again to Micaiah. "He may treat us as the outsiders he believes us to be, but that gives us no right to attack the man. In fact, that may be precisely what he wants us to do. Have you considered that?"

Micaiah was speechless. He hadn't considered that. And, what's more, Johan'an probably hadn't either. And, the more they were allowed to think about this, the more they were all becoming convinced of the necessity of action.

And then, as if an after-thought, Azariah turned to young Micaiah and ordered, "You are to stay here with your sister. If anything happens, I want someone loyal by her side."

But, before Micaiah could argue, a voice broke through from behind, "If anything happens?"

It was Cala, carrying young Samuel. She was wearing the necklace Barak had given her when he made her his bride. Her eyes were afire while her frame stood strong. She seemed ready for anything. Strong. Stronger than ever before. The men standing before her were all taken off guard. They had forgotten, in all the commotion, that Cala's official period of mourning was over.

Johan'an had never been so angry. Usually, he was a man of diplomacy and grace. But, now, he seemed to be quickly shedding those attributes. With every step along his march, he found it harder to hold back the rage. Angry thoughts raced through the disciplined mind of the aspiring patriarch in such a way as to strip him of any vestige of reason.

Of course, Johan'an had never had a member of his family threatened in such a horrid way before, either. Curses of this sort were not to be taken lightly. The mind behind it all belonged to a dangerous man who was capable of carrying out the threats left in front of the tent. Only one name came to mind, yet Johan'an wished somehow he could be wrong. But, he knew he was right. There was no doubt in his mind -- Massoud.

He had already visited Massoud's tent only to find his wife confused and of little or no help. What mattered was Massoud wasn't there, and it was almost daybreak. Johan'an refused to believe that Massoud had gotten up this early to work. Barak's eldest was never much of a worker, but more of a taskmaster -- and a very overbearing one at that. He would probably be the last to rise of the lot of them, and yet he demanded so much respect. What surprised Johan'an most was that there was a faction of Barak's people who looked to Massoud as a leader. The thought of Massoud being in

CHAPTER SIXTEEN

◆ ✚ ◆

A dead quiet settled throughout the crowd. The gruesome act they had just witnessed was something they were totally unaccustomed to seeing. Violence of this sort was just not a part of their calm existence. All present were left speechless. Then, suddenly, a blood-curdling scream broke the quiet. It was the recently widowed Cala. She thought she had known enough grief already. She was sure her pain could not have been worse than that of the past eight days. She found that she was terribly wrong.

Cala broke free of those restraining her, falling upon the lifeless body of her dear father, Johan'an. Massoud saw her coming and had to restrain both the urge to smile and the hunger he had to use the bloody spear on the young woman as well. Instead, he pierced the ground with a thunderous blow and walked away. He then knelt beside the dead body of his brother, Sayed. There were no tears, he was only taking a moment to catch his breath and think.

Micaiah tried desperately to break free and get at Massoud. But the towering figure of Abishur stood ready to block his way and do whatever battle necessary. The young boy had almost worked his way free when Stephanus and Othniel caught his arms and held him tight. They both knew that letting Micaiah go on a berserk attack would do none of them any good. Then, Azariah stepped forward and whispered something in his grandson's ear that seemed to calm him down a little. Unfortunately, it was all the priest could do to compose himself. He found himself subconsciously tearing at his garment again as his tears returned.

Melchior walked past the priest and came to kneel beside Johan'an. Putting a caring hand upon the arm of young Cala, the magus bowed his head in prayer. As Melchior prayed for guidance, he found himself stroking the tiny head of the baby, Samuel, who was resting comfortably in his mother's arms amid the chaos. After what seemed like an eternity, Melchior stood and walked over to the body of Sayed. This time, instead of kneeling, he simply stood and stared at Massoud. Then, as if sensing the accusing eyes of the elder upon him, Massoud looked up to face the wise one.

There were no words between the two, only cold stares. But Melchior could hear the confession of Massoud in every look. The old one returned a stare, just as revealing, *"I know what you did."* it accused.

"What do I care if you do, old man?" Massoud's eyes screamed.

The crime was clear and unveiled to the magus like one of his former dreams. Massoud wanted what was his and killed his brother when there was a threat to stop him. Johan' an had become the scapegoat to his rage. The murderer, Massoud, had orchestrated it all at a moment's notice, but in reality, he had premeditated this crime a thousand times over in his hardened heart. Massoud realized then and there that from then on, his dark soul lay bare to the seer. And he didn't care, because he believed, when it came down to it, Melchior was powerless to stop him.

Then Massoud stood. He filled his lungs with fresh air and savored the moment. He stood alone now. There were none with the power to challenge him. He was now the master of his own destiny as well as the destiny of his people. He took his time, satisfied to soak in the moment. It was obvious to Melchior that Massoud relished all of this. The power, after all, was intoxicating.

Finally, when he decided it was time to get down to business, Massoud looked out across the crowd. *"What sheep!"* he thought, considering his next move as shepherd. And then, the eldest son of the patriarch Barak spoke for the first time as the leader of his people.

"These are dark days that we are forced to live. We have lost our beloved leader, and, now my brother. What is next? What will be taken from us next? We find ourselves betrayed by those we have called friends . . . dare I say, family? But, now their treachery is evident. Their eyes have always been upon our land, our cattle, and our women -- upon us! My father was gracious enough to allow them use of the land of the Wadi-Naklah, and even granted them the land stretching south to the Gabal Musa. But this has now been found inadequate for them. They venture to spread across the hill country by whatever means necessary!"

The crowd stirred with shouts and protests. A few jeered and began to yell epitaphs at Johan'an's family. As the crowd reached the peak of its frenzy, Massoud brought his hand up and the people were quiet again. This response brought exceeding pleasure to the dark heart of Massoud.

"I believe further action is necessary! But, by our own law, this is to be taken up by the council of elders. I am calling a council immediately here in my father's tent in one hour's time." Massoud turned back toward his father's tent when suddenly he caught the eye of the young maid he had had company with not even one hour ago. Neither of them had slept much the night before, but her smile was fresh and inviting. He almost forgot himself right there in front of everyone.

The young maiden's father, Abishur, apparently not very happy with the type of eye contact the two were making, changed the direction of Massoud's rather twisted thoughts. "And what of the other Hebrews?"

Massoud answered, never taking his eyes off the firm body of the maiden, "Put them under guard. Nothing is to happen to them until the council is over. Understand?"

Abishur gave his 'superior' a respectful nod and turned, motioning to four of his kin to help carry the Hebrews away. The first of them to reach Cala tried to grab the young mother by her garment but Stephanus let go of Micaiah long enough to reach out and grab the hand of the herdsman. The two gave each other very posturing stares, yet did nothing for a long moment. Othniel refused to allow Micaiah to break free, although he himself stood ready to defend Melchior's newest project at any cost. And, just when the tension was about to break, Melchior stepped forward and said, "Massoud! I do not believe physical force is necessary. The three of them will come quietly and Stephanus and Othniel will see to that."

Massoud, cringing at the voice of the elder, simply said, "So be it. But, still the guards will be your escorts and your hosts. Do nothing to betray our trust, mind you!"

"There will be no more threatening today, Massoud," Melchior returned, pausing to make eye contact with the murderer again. "I promise."

Turning to Othniel and Stephanus, the elder said simply, "Stay with them and protect them with your very lives. I am staying to see what transpires in this *council*. Once you know where they are being held, send Stephanus to me for further orders."

Othniel shot his master an astonished look. Separated again? Why was he finding himself not at his master's side more and more? It was a position he could never be used to -- a position he could never live with. And yet, it was where he was spending more and more of his time these dark days. Alone. Without his mentor, his master, his friend.

Stephanus stood his ground as the herdsman stood up and backed off, although reluctantly. The lost, young Roman then reached out and helped Cala to her feet and motioned for her to join her brother and grandfather. Micaiah actually appreciated the gesture, and yet he wished he could keep from liking the boy. Azariah gave Melchior a nod with tear-filled eyes and said, "Thank you." As the guards and the prisoners walked off, Melchior turned his attention back to Barak's tent. He never remembered dreading entering the tent so. But, he had also not felt the kind of dark, foreboding evil emanating from the tent, either. Whatever Godliness and holiness Barak bestowed upon the tent and the camp was already beginning to fade. In fact, it may have died with young Sayed.

Before the hour was over, all thirteen elders were present, seated, and had already started a heated discussion of the events of the morning. Each elder had with him his eldest son. There was a time Melchior could look into every face and see the future of Barak's people shining with hope. But all he could see now was despair and darkness.

The elders were split into two distinct groups. The majority were truly elders, aged and wise. The other groups were as young as Massoud, and as rash and simple-minded, too. Falah, who had voiced his opinion the night before, seemed to be a leader among the younger group. Only Abishur kept his distance from this group of young, hungry wolves. The true elders were the majority of the group, eight in all, but they couldn't be expected to stand as one now that Barak was gone. All Melchior could do now upon was pray. No dreams or signs or visions of the future. Only prayer.

Many of the older ones came and spoke to Melchior out of respect. The magus had been in all their tents; interpreted their dreams; read from the scriptures; sought God's will in every one of their lives; and had even seen to the births of some of their children. The fact was that Melchior had delivered most of the young men who made up the other part of the elders. But, after the death of their fathers, Melchior spent less and less time in the tents of their people. It made him wonder what kind of leaders they were to be. And, as Massoud appeared with his wife and eldest son, still but a toddler, Melchior knew he was about to find out.

A royal court was obviously coming into session with solemn graveness. Melchior almost broke a grin at the thought. Massoud was milking this moment for all it was worth, appearing with all the garments, ornaments and items of royalty. He made sure all thirteen elders had their chance to show their subservience to his 'royal honor', never looking any of them eye to eye.

By the time Massoud finally took the seat that had once belonged to his father, Melchior, among others, had had enough of this flaunting of power. For as soon as all was quiet, the eldest of them all, Jared, spoke cuttingly and to the point, "I am uncertain as to why you see it necessary to enter this meeting with such ceremony. Nor do I understand the rashness or the manner in which you executed 'justice' without consulting any of us. The death of Johan'an was simply unnecessary, guilty or not!"

All heads turned immediately to Massoud. If he was attempting -- a rather weak word for what the devil was up to -- to usurp power, this was definitely an attempt by Jared to challenge him. Massoud kept his head about him and said with a tinge of resentment, "Unnecessary? I saw my bother die with my own eyes at the tip of a spear which was a gift to my father by these traitorous exiles! I believe my actions were quite sane."

"Sane or not, Johan'an was a man respected among our ranks. I believe he was due a civil hearing at least, not sacrificed to some ancient, outdated law of 'blood vengeance.' I thought our people were beyond that sort of thing."

Massoud, attempting to compose himself, gave the elder, Jared, a stern, unwavering look and said, "And I thought their people were beyond such treachery. It looks as if we were all wrong."

Another older member, Eben, raised his staff, and questioned, "Even if we are to believe Johan'an capable of such evil, there is little evidence to support this paranoid delusion that his people, our kin, are plotting against us! I am sorry, I am unconvinced," he added with a sarcastic laugh.

Massoud stood, still controlling his rage, yet visibly irritated. "I saw Johan'an's evil with my own eyes and heard of his people's treachery with my own ears. I stand on my word that if we do not act quickly, our lives will all be in danger."

There was a rumbling from the assembly as the young Falah rose to support Massoud. "I have witnessed it also. I have heard their whisperings. Their lust for our land is insatiable."

The rumble became a full fledged riot. Arguments broke out amongst them all. The division was becoming quite clear, and Massoud couldn't have been happier.

"Quiet!!" A voice was raised above the rabble. It was Caled, one of the oldest ones. "I too have seen their looks and heard their grumbling. Their numbers grow yearly, and, soon, they will overtake us all. Once our people were a proud lot. We controlled the Arabian coastline up to the peninsula once called the land of Midian. Our trusting ways have not served us well, though. One nation after another has taken from us. We find our peoples splintered and fractioned and, worst of all, integrated into their races. And, here we are, huddled in fear -- ready to give ourselves to another nation because of trust. Well, I for one say let them go back to where they came from."

A cry of approval arose from the elders. But, a few of them remained silent, unmoved. Abishur, the burly herdsman, carried a look of confusion about him. He wasn't sure where to stand, and yet he knew soon he would be forced into a decision.

Massoud could wait no longer. He finally regained the attention of all attending and began to place his malevolent plot before them all. "It is clear to me that the murder of my brother is, quite simply, an act of war upon our people. Their actions have betrayed their dark hearts, and so I have come to the conclusion that our response should be a response of war!"

There were no shouts. There were no cheers. No one but Massoud seemed to see this turn of events coming, and no one knew what to say next.

CHAPTER SEVENTEEN

⋄ ✦ ⋄

"War?" A faint voice broke the silence, and the weakened form of Eben, tribes eldest, seemed shaken just at the mention of the word. "Has it really come to that?"

"I am afraid it has, Eben. I am afraid it has." Massoud spoke, realizing that he had all their attention now. He had dreamed of this moment -- just last evening. And now all his dreams seemed to be coming true. But, for some present, this was nothing close to a dream. It was reality and a nightmare all wrapped up together.

Melchior couldn't believe his own ears, yet he could see it coming a mile off. It was everything the magus could do just to restrain his emotion and not cry out. He alone knew the truth. He also knew that he was powerless against the darkness coming. He could protest, yet it wasn't his place. They were the ones forced into this terrible decision. And, if they still sided with Massoud after his declaring war, there was nothing Melchior could say to dissuade them. But, before any discussions could begin, Massoud brought the "resolution" quickly to the table.

"We have wasted enough time! The Hebrews have moved onto our land and tainted the memory of our departed leader. They want all we have and they are willing to kill to get it. I say we bring it to a council vote. I say we consider raising a war party and chasing the Hebrews out of the hill country, taking back the land our fathers worked so hard for, and making them pay for their evil intentions. Who is with me?"

This was sudden silence. A good measure of tension filled the room. Melchior almost protested again, but kept silent. The elders looked at each other, waiting for someone to make a move one way or another. Suddenly, quickly, Falah was on his feet.

"Our clan is with you! I say war!" Falah raised his fist and four others stood. Akiva, Amoz, and Davin were expected. They were young and followed Falah and Massoud like school boys. But one of the men standing had not been heard from yet. His name was Bononi.

Bononi was a middle-aged man with a strong and rugged nature. His presence was felt quickly, though his voice was always soft. He had both kept silent and to himself during most of the gathering. He had listened to the words of those around him and now he was forced to speak.

"My father opposed giving the Hebrews land in the first place. And, now that he is gone, and I have lived to see the contempt they have shown us, I must agree. The time for talk and charity must end. Only strength will give answer to what they have done."

Melchior tried to reassure himself that there was no way Massoud would gain a majority among such a wise assembly. He was convinced of this until another stood to join the war-hawks. It was the bitter, old Caled. *Of course*, Melchior thought, *He has been full of anger for generations. His clan's numbers began to dwindle in the shadow of the Hebrews blessed explosion of growth, and Caled has murmured and grumbled ever since. Malicious old fool!*

But there were only six standing, and to gain support for his intentions, Massoud needed seven. Melchior whispered a quick prayer for Almighty God to somehow block the evil one's plan. Surely this was not the will of God to see Barak's, and Azariah's, people at such odds. Then, as Melchior opened his eyes in "Amen," he saw two more standing.

To his relief, the two new supporters were not elders, but first sons of the two most prominent leaders of largest clans in the hill country. Melchior's relief turned to shock as the eldest of the two, Moshae began to speak. "I cannot withstand my father's silence any longer. Legally, it is not my place, but I, and many of my clan, are ready, even now, to take up arms against those who have attacked us."

Moshae's aged father, Eben, turned to him, embarrassed and disgraced. "Sit down, Moshae." He then turned to Massoud. "Not one of my clan will participate in such an evil venture. God convict you all of what you suggest. War, indeed!"

Moshae refused to sit, or even look at his father eye-to-eye, but continued, "I am sorry, Father. I respect your words, but I must stand with Massoud on this; and there are many of our people who will follow me despite your orders."

The other man who stood was Thanor, who was not the first born of Kadam's family, but the oldest surviving son. Kadam stood, but not to join his son. Instead, the father looked the son straight in the eye and was dumbfounded. He could see that Thanor was also ready to dishonor him and follow Massoud into battle. His son's actions brought tears to his weary eyes, and he found he could do nothing more than sit out of shame.

But, still there wasn't a seventh elder. There still was a chance to evade such darkness. Melchior found himself praying harder and stronger, and, at times, out loud. The sound of the magus' prayers annoyed Massoud greatly, mainly because he knew that the petitions weren't for him.

"I count eight standing. That comprises most of the camp. What of the rest of you?" Massoud stopped, breathless.

Eben gave him a hateful look and said, "My word still counts and stands. No matter what my son says, or does, I still speak for my clan! And I say, no!"

"I concur!" was all Kadam could say, still crying, broken and confused. *Four against,* thought Melchior, *Come now, surely there are others . . .*

And there were others -- or at least *one* other. The stone-faced Hananel spoke to the point and voiced what surely others in the tent were thinking. "Massoud, I must speak candidly. I respected your father, Barak. We all did. And your brother, Sayed, was a man of honor and truth." Then Hananel stopped and brought up from within his soul what he felt must be said, "But you, young man, have never struck me as one I would allow to lead me into any situation, much less battle."

Massoud and Hananel were now locked eye-to-eye in a silent, spiritual combat. Oh, how Massoud wished he could strike the old fool. But he knew that was totally unnecessary. The old crone would learn soon enough not to challenge him. All the others who had stood in Massoud's way weren't here to tell the tale. And Massoud made sure Hananel knew that he wouldn't long be either, just by the look he was giving the elder. Nonetheless, Hananel finished, "You will excuse me for not taking your word for the events of the morning, but I refuse to believe Johan'an capable of murder. And, as for his people, there is no treachery going on here, only the workings of a paranoid mind -- a mind I never chose as leader!"

A look of shock was on every face. Even if they had thought what Hananel had just said, they would have never voiced it. Massoud looked the most shocked of all. For a time, there was no answer, and Melchior hoped that that was the end of it. But Massoud was never short on words, "I respect your position, Hananel. And, needless to say, we have never been friends -- but that still gives you no right to question me or call me a liar before the elders. If you have a personal problem with me, we will discuss it in private. If you wish to challenge my word, my honor," Massoud hesitated, "bring proof!"

Massoud secretly smiled, knowing there would be no such proof. He then looked at the eight men still standing firm and continued,

"Now. There are two elders we have not heard from, and by the looks of it, your word will decide our actions."

Abishur still looked confused. War was an extreme response to anything, but what if Massoud and the others were right. They would end up fighting for their land, anyway. But no! His words from the night before came back to strengthen his resolve. For no matter what had been said, Abishur knew that Johan'an and his kin were good people. And there was no way he would believe them capable of murder or instigating war.

"I say no!" Abishur decreed. "I believe if we attack the Hebrews, we will be acting upon our emotions and not out of logic and reason. I don't believe we have all the facts."

Melchior's heart leaped with joy! The count was six to six, and the tide seemed to be turning. Maybe the day had been saved after all.

Then, El'hanan stood, not saying a word, but all present knew his decision by the way he looked at Barak's surviving son. As a deadening chill filled the tent, Massoud smiled.

CHAPTER EIGHTEEN

◆ ✚ ◆

E *l'hanan had chosen war.*
The debate raged on, but Melchior heard nothing. His mind was frozen in absolute horror and disbelief. At sunrise, he had come to grips with his mortality. But the louder the argument grew, the wearier he became. He had also thought himself ready to face the task set before him. The star. The journey. The birth of hope itself.

But the enemy was on the move again, as he always was. Now, there were two more men to mourn. And, what made matters worse was that Melchior knew the monster that committed both atrocious acts. His name was Massoud, and he had just successfully stirred the once peaceful residents of the hill country to war against an innocent people. And there was absolutely nothing the magus could do to stop him.

To Massoud's dismay, there was still an argument going on amongst the elders. He really thought when he gained a majority, the matter would be settled and the whole of Barak's people would immediately prepare for war. Not so. The seven clan leaders who sided with Massoud were ready enough for war. Even the two rebel sons seemed sure they could rally a majority of their people. However, the remaining four clan leaders absolutely refused to go along.

Massoud set off into a berserk-like reign of condemnation against all who refused *his* majority rule even though he really believed that it wouldn't matter. Between the seven clan leaders and the two rebel sons, he was sure he could rally a clear cut majority. Still, a challenge was a challenge -- one Massoud couldn't stomach at this time.

The six dissenting elders pushed their peaceful resolutions harder and harder. Still, there was nothing they could say or do to sway these hungry wolves that were ready for war. Who were they kidding? They have been ready for a confrontation since Barak allowed the Hebrews on their land. This was just waiting to happen. And, without proper leadership, there was no stopping it.

Melchior had tried to return to his prayers, but found no words of petition adequate. He fought with all his strength to keep from falling into that dark pit of despair that overcame him earlier. The magus found himself trying desperately to block out the arguments of the council, and yet they flooded his soul and threatened the sanity of his mind. That is when Stephanus returned and gave Melchior a chance to leave the tent without causing a scene.

Once Stephanus and Melchior had escaped the pandemonium of the council tent, the young Roman reported, "The others were taken back to the guest tent -- where the etchings were."

Melchior knew that even though the curse in the sand was long gone, the threat was alive and well. That dark lion from his dream was encircling the encampment. He could hear him. Feel him. That all too familiar chill. The one you feel just before something horrible is about to happen. The elder couldn't fathom anything more horrible than the acts committed within the recent day. All he knew was that things were about to get worse.

"What in the world is going on in there?" Stephanus broke the silence, confused.

"War!" Melchior said, with solemn face.

"War? But that is ridiculous!" Stephanus almost laughed.

"I am afraid it is quite serious, Stephen. There may be a need to make escape plans. But I am not leaving Johan'an's kin in the hands of that monster, Massoud!"

Stephanus didn't even attempt to correct Melchior concerning his name this time. He was glad enough to hear the magus' resolve to leave. He was willing to do whatever was necessary, to get as far away from this place as possible. Personally, he knew of no other way out of the hill country or Muza. The magus seemed to be the only way for him to return home.

"I don't see any reason to stay here any longer. Come, son, let us make good our escape."

Before Melchior could finish his plans, a hulking figure burst through the tent door. It was Abishur, and he didn't look happy. "Massoud would like to see you, Melchior." And with that, the young 'elder' bounded off in the direction they had taken Azariah.

"What was that about? And where is he going?" asked Stephanus.

"I am not sure, my son. I must go and see what Massoud wants. Is there a way you can get back to Othniel without Abishur seeing you?"

"Of course! He may be bigger, but I am faster," Stephanus said with a smile.

"Well, go and warn Othniel that all does not go well here. Tell him to be ready to act no matter what Abishur does. Now go!"

Stephanus took off like a shot and left Melchior wondering what Massoud was up to now. As the magus neared the tent, Hananel and Jared emerged more than furious. Hananel stopped and touched Melchior's shoulder and said, "I am truly sorry old friend. I never thought it would ever come to this. Needless to say, I miss Barak more than ever now!"

With that, Hananel walked off toward his tent. Melchior had been there many times, and had come to respect the elder almost as much as he had Barak. Almost. Next to leave the tent was the frail form of Eben. All he could do was shake his head and say, "What that boy is doing will not only spill much blood, but will set clan against clan -- civil unrest unmeasured in our long, illustrious history. Whatever integrity our people may have built in millennia, he will destroy in days."

As Eben walked off, trusting his walking stick a mite too much, Melchior thought, "Prophetic? Lord, I hope not!" Then, the other two, Ariel and Kadam, passed Melchior as he re-entered the tent. Massoud was waiting -- and his smile was unusually wide.

It had begun to get dark and Stephanus was trying hard not to get lost among the sea of tents. This day had seemed to go exceptionally quickly, but it wasn't due to the fun he was having, that was sure. With every turn, the boy became more and more fearful. But he simply couldn't let Melchior down. The magus was counting on him to relay the message to his servant, Othniel.

"Now that could not have been expected!" said Stephanus to himself. "Since when did I even care what my own father thought about me -- much less some stranger?"

The thought of his father sobered him up quite suddenly. For, although he and his father never quite got along, every boy loves his father to some degree, and Stephanus was no exception to the rule.

Stephanus' father was an important man about the courts of Rome. The Senate moved daily to increase the boundaries of their mighty empire, but Arabia had always eluded them. His father had been an essential agent dealing with the lands south of Judea. He had been finishing negotiations with leaders up and down the coastline of the Red Sea when their paths crossed with the cutthroat, Bassam.

Stephanus remembers his father saying that the only reason he brought him along was to expose him to the workings of government.

"After all," his father said, "the boy has to learn to do *something* with his life, doesn't he? This way, he can begin his journey into manhood with experience!" Surely, his father hadn't expected the events of the past week or so to happen the way they had. It was certain that this was not what he had in mind as 'experience.'

Nonetheless, 'experience' it was. And Stephanus was having to grow up quickly and become a man long before he had wished to. It wasn't even two months ago that he and his brothers had played along the shores of the great sea and ventured to the Coliseum to catch a glimpse of a real gladiator -- both things expected of boys at play. But Stephanus, like it or not, was to become a man by being a part of some grand adventure even he couldn't imagine. He definitely wouldn't have chosen it this way, but he couldn't turn back now. There were too many lives counting on him and too much at stake.

Suddenly, Stephanus realized that he hadn't been paying attention to where he was going. He was lost -- sort of. He had just straightened his direction out and turned another corner around *another* tent, when a shadow seemed to envelope him and grab a hold of him. The 'shadow' was Abishur! And he didn't seem all that happy to see Stephanus.

Melchior approached Massoud cautiously, carefully, never breaking eye contact. Massoud's usual look of contempt was now mixed with a swelling of personal pride. He waited patiently as the magus eased into view. The two had never liked one another, as much enemies as darkness and light. But, ceremony had forced the two together. A common bond loosely held one reluctantly to the other -- namely, the people of the hill country. But, where Melchior had come to love and direct this people, Massoud was bent on using them to succeed in his evil dreams. The two were destined to collide. And by the looks of it, the 'collision' had begun.

Chapter Nineteen

◆ ✚ ◆

Micaiah had never been so outraged. As far as he could tell, his people had never been so insulted. Such an abomination that Massoud should seek to implicate his people in such an insidious plot when it was obvious that the evil plotter was Massoud himself. Above and beyond all that, Massoud was also a murderer. Micaiah couldn't erase the images of the spear plunging into his father's heart. Nor could he keep from hearing Johan'an's last breath. And try as he might to subdue it, the anger continued to boil within him.

Azariah, too, was in shock, but from the outside none could tell. The calm of age and wisdom settled upon him as he sought after God's place amid all the chaos. Othniel stood patiently, overseeing them all with a steady gaze and arms folded. If one didn't know better, he would think that the gentle giant was one of the guards. But his concerned demeanor would surely give him away -- that and the reaction he would get from the real guards whenever he would stick his head out of the tent entrance.

But the calmest among them seemed to be Cala. Her head told her to fear her future, but her heart was full of faith. Cala's father, Johan' an, and grandfather, Azariah, both instilled the proper religious principles in her by simply being the men of God they were called to be. But her short life with the elder Barak also taught her to have faith in all circumstances. It was almost as if she had been prepared to handle just such a tragedy. And, even if the 'reality' of life proved too much for her, one look into the eyes of her dear baby, Samuel, and she couldn't help but be hopeful.

Micaiah had had just about enough. He grabbed Azariah's walking staff -- a sturdy piece of wood for its age -- and headed for the entrance. He was met there by Othniel, who did nothing more than block his way, saying, "And where do you think you are going?"

Their eyes met and Micaiah's heart almost melted. He turned his eyes slowly away, and then, suddenly, regained his courage. But before he could strike the unmovable giant, his grandfather's voice rang out, "Micaiah!" The young, angry man froze, "Sit down!" And with that, he retreated to find a seat.

There were no other words. The hopelessness and helplessness of their situation was more evident than ever. Micaiah sank into overwhelming surrender. Othniel took yet another look to see if Melchior was coming with good news, to no avail. Azariah and Cala both knew that only God could change their situation now. And as Samuel slept peacefully in his mother's arms, there were suddenly voices at the entrance of the tent.

"Come closer, Magus," said Massoud, in an unnerving tone, "We have much to discuss."

With that, Melchior knew the rest of their conversation would be rather unpleasant. Nonetheless, the aged wise man came closer and found the seat granted him just to Massoud's left. "*The left,*" he thought, "*how fitting!*"

As Melchior got comfortable, he spoke out of respect and ceremony, as if Barak were still in the seat of authority. "I, Melchior, humble servant to the Almighty God of our forefathers, whose steadfast love and care has kept us both, am now at your disposal."

Massoud, a bit surprised at the magus' show of respect, collected himself and resumed his agenda. "Yes, yes! Thank you for coming, Melchior. As you know, we are in a very awkward situation here. And, at the risk of sounding vindictive, I feel that someone must pay the price for my brother's murder."

At that, the magus shot a very knowing glance back at Massoud and repeated, "Yes. Someone *must* pay."

Massoud ignored the magus and went on, "It is the decision of the council of elders that the actions of the Hebrew peoples to the north are paramount to an act of war. Therefore, I feel we must react in kind."

The stares between the two had become stronger and more intense. They both knew the others thoughts, but continued anyway. "If the council has voted this, so be it," Melchior retorted.

Massoud smiled as Melchior continued to stare, "Yes. We have decided to go to war immediately, as to not lose the element of surprise, which brings me to you, Melchior."

"And, now," the magus thought, *"we have finally arrived at the point of this whole gathering."* And, as Massoud stood, it was obvious that he was going to 'come to the point'.

With a ceremonious tone and a sanctimonious grin, Massoud summed it all up. "We seek the blessing due us as we go to war. And the only person among us that can deliver this 'blessing' is you, Magus!"

The voices from outside, although indistinguishable, had not escaped the notice of all who were waiting in the tent. Micaiah stood expectantly when Othniel motioned for him to stay put as the giant leaned to the entrance listening. Othniel could make out the voice of the clan elder, Abishur. The conversation seemed formal and to the point; something about another prisoner. But before the magus' servant could look to see who was being imprisoned, the tent flap opened and Stephanus came rolling abruptly to a stop at Othniel's feet. The one responsible for rolling the young man was, of course, Abishur, who had stepped into the tent and was even now eye to eye with Othniel.

There was a terrible silence, and then, when Abishur was sure the tent entrance was closed and the guards were gone, he reached into his cloak and smiled. What he brought out was a mace and, at first, Micaiah was sure a brawl was about to break out. Suddenly, Abishur turned the handle toward Othniel and said, "Take this! We must leave here *now!*"

"A blessing?" Melchior replied, a bit puzzled. "You seek a blessing?"

Massoud was still standing and smiling even bigger, although not as sincerely as before. Without looking the magus in the face, he returned, "Yes. A blessing. Do you think we would go to war without the proper rituals? A blessing is always sought in distressing times. It is law."

Melchior knew this, of course. What astonished him was that Massoud knew the law and was actually playing this whole thing according to the rules. The magus thought for a second and then replied, quickly in realization, "I cannot simply *give* you a blessing, Massoud. It does not work like that."

Massoud now turned to face the magus with a flushed, angry look and asked, "Why not?"

Melchior half-smiled and explained, "I am a priest and prophet, of sorts, and although I stand between your people and the Most High, I cannot speak such a thing without approaching our God and seeking His word on your plans, Massoud. My blessing would be of no use to you."

Massoud calmed down a bit and replied, "Oh. Of course. Well, how much time is required?"

Melchior planted his walking stick and raised himself to stand toe-to-toe with Massoud, "One does not rush God, Massoud, but I will go to the high place and call upon the Most High's holy name on behalf of your people. After He speaks to me, and only after He speaks to me, will I return with an answer."

Massoud was now close enough to the magus to breathe on his face. The two were still giving each other those 'knowing' glances. It was obvious now that Massoud was attempting to force Melchior to choose sides. Melchior could only give him what God gave him. Nothing more.

Massoud turned and gave the magus an ultimatum. "Fine. You go to the high place and return with God's blessing in due time. But, mind you, Magus, time is of the essence and, for your friends, time is extremely short."

It was then that Melchior realized the dilemma before him. Massoud expected a blessing, and quickly. He was willing to threaten the magus, even in front of the elders, in order to get it. And, although he suspected the answer, it now fell upon him to search the will of God in the midst of this chaos for a blessing Melchior could never give.

CHAPTER TWENTY

◆ ✚ ◆

T he starless darkness seemed to blanket the land as Abishur readied the small group for escape. The plan was simple -- overwhelm the guards and make haste through the night to the place where Abishur kept a group of prize horses. Camels were the usual mode of transportation in the hill country, but this situation called for more speed.

Othniel and Abishur made quick work of the guards and led the way. Although they should have been grateful, Micaiah and Stephanus both had ill feeling about missing the chance to get their shots in. Incredible as it may sound, the plan went off without complication. They encountered no one and had no trouble reaching the horses. But once there, they found that their plan was incomplete.

"Take the horses and flee from here quickly. There is no time to lose," Abishur said, looking around to make sure they weren't spotted.

As some of the others were mounting their horses, Abishur noticed that Othniel was missing. Turning around, he caught a glimpse of the giant's form in the torch light. He was just standing there with his back to the others. Abishur was beginning to get worried and said, "Come on, Othniel. You escape now or never!"

Othniel never turned around, but kept staring into the heart of the hills around him. "I cannot leave without my master!"

Abishur, trying to be understanding, replied, "Do you want to die? If we are caught, Massoud is just crazy enough to have us all executed. It is imperative we leave now!"

Othniel never changed his tone, and he never moved, but repeated dryly, "I will not leave without Melchior! Had I realized that was part of your plan, I would never have come along!"

Stephanus, who had just mounted his horse, broke in, realizing Othniel's point, "He is right. We cannot just leave Melchior at Massoud's mercy. There can't be much mercy left in him."

Abishur, frustrated, replied, trying to keep his voice down, "And what do you suggest we do, boy, attack Massoud in the heart of the camp and rescue the holy man? Why, we would never make it out alive."

"Someone has to rescue him. It would be dishonorable to leave him and run like cowards," Micaiah stepped in.

"Do you forget, Hebrew, what happened to your father, and what is about to happen to all your people? Someone has to warn them, too. If you die for honor here, what hope is there for any of your people?"

Abishur was looking around now, expecting a search party any minute.

Azariah touched Abishur on the arm and said calmly, "Young man, there are other things we have not taken into consideration." Abishur gave him a questioning look and the elder went on, "The young mother and child cannot survive a race along the hill country, and I am also too weary to suffer a journey at such a pace."

"What are you suggesting, Azariah? If we ride by camel, we will be overtaken. Listen, all of you," Abishur now looked quite frantic. "We have a short time to get out of here. One bit of hesitation and we risk detection. And if we are detected, there is nothing but death left for any of us!"

With that, it seemed everything was at a stalemate. Othniel would not budge and Azariah seemed unwilling to race home. And, between the two was Abishur, who was about at the end of his rope and beginning to wish he had never helped them at all. But, before anyone could speak, a song rose across the hill country; a song sung by a voice that Othniel recognized immediately. And, as an unusual fire in the high places lit up the night, Othniel looked with awesome hope and said, "Melchior!"

It was a song his father had taught him -- a song of the psalms. It was a song Melchior always seemed to turn to when faced with an impossible task. He had sung it before leaving his dead family in the desert to seek life as a magus's assistant. He had sung it after the death of his beloved wife. Melchior had sung it many times while attempting to raise Othniel with the morals and virtue he had been taught to live by. And he had sung it just days before while mourning the death of his dearest friend, Barak. And, of course, he found himself singing it again.

The 'impossible task' set before the magus concerned a blessing he knew he couldn't give. And, what's more, Massoud KNEW he would never give such a blessing. This made Melchior wonder what Massoud could possibly hope to gain by forcing this confrontation. The elder once again forced himself to try and put such questions out of his mind. It had been hours since he had set his face to God in search for the Almighty's word. Finally, in absolute surrender, Melchior threw himself literally prostrate before God. While waiting for the Most High's voice to break through, the magus drifted off to sleep.

When Melchior woke up, he was still surrounded by the dark of night. But the noise that shook him from his dreamless slumber seemed to be coming from the trail that led up from the camp. There had been two guards within sight of Melchior at all times. Massoud, it seemed, didn't quite trust him. But now, the guards had been joined by a torch-bearing mob and Melchior began to fear for his safety. Then, suddenly, an unspeakable calm rushed over him and he found himself in the grasp of supernatural hands.

It was the sight of Massoud leading the angry group that should have caused fear, but Melchior suddenly felt an overwhelming, sickening anger. Massoud stopped short of stepping onto the holy place, and spouted hatefully, "Your friends, the Hebrews, have fled, taking Othniel, the boy and one of our misguided elders with them. It seems they may have been gone for several hours, their absence only being detected by the change of guard. We find it imperative to arm ourselves and assault the Hebrew encampment as soon as possible. So, you see, we have come for your answer!"

The magus felt an incredible urge to strike the young tyrant down and also felt he would be absolutely justified in doing so. Then, he began to realize that these 'feelings' were not all his own. They seemed to be the emotions and reactions of a separate entity. He had been in the 'grasp' of this supernatural entity before. It was then that Melchior let his will be absolutely subjugated by the spirit and will of Almighty God. Through His spokesman, the word of God came, "Massoud, son of the faithful and just Barak, you attempt to raise yourself beyond the heights that Almighty God assigns to you. His word came and stands concerning who will lead your people. Barak's son, Samuel, received his father's blessing and, therefore, the blessing of Almighty God. But now you wage war against Jacob and set your sights upon the wealth of Israel's sons. You ask for a blessing and, therefore, ask me to curse the seed of Israel. How can I curse whom God has not cursed? And, likewise, how can I bless whom God is unwilling to bless? Behold, I have received a command to bless, but God's eternal blessing stands with Jacob and Israel, and not with you. The Lord their God is with them. There are no signs of divination that can make me bless you and not them. For it was the Lord our God that said, 'Blessed be everyone who blesses you, and cursed be everyone who curses you.' The oracle of Melchior, son of Amoz, son of Ben-Aray, son of the High Priest Thias, the oracle of the man whose eyes are opened. The oracle of him who hears the words of God. The seed of Israel has the blessing and I cannot revoke it. Turn from this spirit of war or you and all who follow will face the wrath of God!"

There was a sudden murmur throughout the crowd. Much of the mob was the young 'dog soldiers' Massoud had wrapped around his little finger. The others consisted of the eldest sons of the elders who had stood with Massoud's war plans, yet they seemed to be a bit shaken at this prophecy. The young warlord then dared to set his unholy foot upon the high place and shake his fist in the face of God. "How dare you! I asked for your blessing and you gave it to my enemy? How is it you expect to live after doing such a thing, Magus? You claim to speak the mind of God? I believe it is obvious whose mind you are speaking. Well, the Hebrews may be your kin, but they are no kin of mine! And, if you are standing with them, then you stand opposed to me. I should have expected as much!"

With this, Massoud turned away, fuming, but hiding a sinister smile.

Melchior was unmoved and repeated, "Turn from this war or you and your war party will be destroyed."

Massoud chose to ignore him and walked away. He was met by the Elder El'hanan, whose resolve seemed a bit shaken. "Surely you don't intend to go against the Hebrews after hearing THAT, do you?"

Massoud stopped and eyed El'hanan with a contemptuous look. "That is precisely what I intend!"

"But the oracle . . ."

The words were no sooner out of El'hanan's mouth when Massoud sprang upon the elder verbally, "The 'oracle' the old magus just spouted is nothing more than the words of his friends, the Hebrews. They intend to use our own religion against us!"

Melchior had found himself leaning up against a rock and looking for somewhere to sit. He had never felt so drained in his life, physically or spiritually. All he knew was that he had just been used of God in such a way that his whole being was taken over by the spirit of God himself. He, once again, denounced Massoud, "I never speak for myself, Massoud. In times such as these, it is the word of the Almighty that I speak, nothing more!"

Massoud turned, almost laughing, "We shall see, shall we not? Either I and my 'war party' never return and you are justified, or I return victorious and you are exposed for the fraud you are. We shall see which, shall we not!?"

Melchior, visibly weakened, could only say in contempt, "We shall see."

Massoud began barking orders and commands immediately. Men darted off to different parts of the camp, readying the troops for war. There was a rally horn blown in the distance and Massoud began to realize a life-long dream.

As Massoud stepped onto the base of the hills, a hand grabbed his shoulder. "Our land and rights are one thing, Massoud. But what you are doing here smacks of heresy." The Elder Bononi now stood eye-to-eye with Massoud and stopped the eager 'general' in his tracks, "I know I agreed to war, but I cannot go against the word of the Almighty!"

Massoud couldn't believe his ears. "You accept the words of the magician?" he asked as he tried to move on and ignore the old man.

Bononi finally got Massoud to slow down long enough to hear his answer. "I have never seen in him anything but honesty and godliness. His words have always been heeded and always his prophecies have come true. It would be death to ignore him now!"

Massoud was definitely becoming angered. To him, these interruptions were uncalled for! The young warlord stopped cold and looked around at his other 'allies.' "All right. How many of you share Bononi's feelings? Come on now! I need to know who my friends are!"

And, although none of this had anything to do with friendship, he could see it in their faces; he had few friends in the group. Bononi walked off, El'hanan and Caled following. Even Falah looked shaken. The youngest of them all, Akiva by name, began to walk off and gave Massoud a defeated look.

But, as he passed Massoud, he suddenly found himself in the grip of very angry hands. Massoud nearly had the young man in a choke hold as he yelled, "No! That is not the end of it!"

Everyone stopped and stared as Massoud realized what he was doing and let the man go. He quickly composed himself and gave an alarming ultimatum. "This is not over! Even as we speak, our people prepare for battle. Listen to them! They thirst for war, revenge flowing through their veins. We cannot stop what has begun!" Massoud turned to the oldest of the elders, "You cannot stop what has begun. You hide behind the words of that treasonous magus to mask your fear and cowardice. But, your sons and grandsons stand ready to save the name and reputation of all your clans!"

No one spoke, allowing Massoud's words to sink in. It was all becoming too clear. Massoud began to walk off and Falah spoke out, a bit puzzled, "So we are still going to war with the Hebrews?"

Massoud spun around and let out a burst of pent up steam and then replied, "Is my brother not still dead? Has my father spawned a Hebrew half-breed that they intend to put over us all as lord and master! By all that is holy, yes, we are going to war!"

Massoud was now panting like he had run a great distance. He looked over the small assembly with greed and contempt. And, then, when he could catch his breath, he went on, "And what is more, when I return victorious, all those who opposed me will be stripped of their power. Their clans will be given to others of *my* choosing. But those who stand with me will rule valiantly over their clans! But you must choose quickly. We leave at sunrise."

He stomped off and then, as an after-thought, he looked back at Melchior, "Oh yes, Melchior! You will be held here until my return. Guards! Let nothing happen to the old man until I return. I will deal out his sentence personally for his act of treason. And, if he escapes, the guards are to be executed!"

Large hands grabbed the frail arms of the elder as he was led away. Melchior believed what he had said was from God, but he couldn't help but wonder whether he had done the right thing.

CHAPTER TWENTY ONE

◆ ✚ ◆

I n the end, he was by far the best and only choice. Someone had to go to the Hebrew encampment and warn them as quickly as possible, and, although most of the others knew the way better, Stephanus proved to be the best trained rider among them. If he had his choice, he would have rather stayed with the others and gone back to Muza. But he knew that Micaiah would not leave his family, and that none of them had learned horsemanship from the best Rome had to offer.

So Stephanus found himself on horseback, racing along the hill country, bearing straight north and praying that his speed was enough.

Micaiah still was unsure about the arrangements. Sure, he loved his sister and grandfather dearly, but to trust the fate of their people with an outsider seemed chancy at best. Yet, he knew his own skill on horseback was lacking for the situation at hand and his family needed him anyway. So, uneasily, he had resolved himself to leading the way to Muza.

The pace was much too slow for any of their likings, and every moment they found themselves with their ears to the wind and their eyes always watching their backs. Even Azariah, the pillar of peace, seemed disturbed. This whole episode with Massoud had all of them on edge. The only sound was the cry of young Samuel, who also seemed to sense the fear and apprehension around him.

"Do you think everything has gone all right with Melchior?" asked Cala, as she tried to calm the baby down.

Azariah looked to the lightening blue sky, and said, "I pray it has. Their fates are in the hands of the living God now. It will be morning soon and much harder to escape without being detected. But, I trust in the steadfast love and care of the Almighty to the end."

Micaiah found himself involuntarily saying, "Amen!" to that as he pressed on toward Muza.

Melchior found himself being hurried along into the heart of the encampment. The lights and sounds of the preparation for battle were all around. People ran to and fro, carrying all sorts of weapons and shields, armor and other gear. Anger and hatred were upon every face, and every voice seemed all too ready to shout epitaphs. The two guarding him never spoke and never stopped. Hoods covered their heads, and their faces were only visible in silhouette.

The threesome turned a corner and almost plowed into a two fully armed warriors, who never gave the three of them any thought and continued on their way. In an attempt to dodge them, all three men lost their footing and fell toward the ground. But before Melchior hit the ground, one of the guards braced him and took most of the impact himself. Melchior could only stare into the shadows of the hood and say, "Othniel?"

The answer came from the darkness, "Yes, Master!"

"It is you, my son! Why, I should have known."

The two embraced in a moment of hope and joy at being reunited. As Othniel removed his hood, tears were streaking down his strong, massive face. "I could not leave without you! To whom would I go?"

The magus could only answer in a thankful embrace. God had spoken through him and God was now helping him escape harm. Suddenly, Melchior began to feel a little ashamed of ever doubting. It wasn't the first time and, of course; it wouldn't be the last.

"This is touching and all, but our lives are still in danger here, you know. You had just better hope that Massoud stays busy with his little war, or we will all pay."

Othniel, a bit angered, replied, "Abishur! Your faith and courage really leave a bit to be desired."

Abishur, not a bit bothered by the giant's words answered, "Faith! Courage! They all have their place, young one. But, there is also a time for careful, fearful diligence. And you could use a bit of that yourself!"

As Othniel helped Melchior to his feet, the magus touched both men on their arms and said, "Both of you are right. Now is the time to flee this place. I am not sure what evil Massoud is about to bring upon this camp, but I do know I have no desire to be here when God's wrath sets down upon the hill country."

Othniel and Melchior actually began to move on, but Abishur stopped them and said, horrified, "Wise one, do you see God's wrath extending to all the camp?"

Melchior never answered. He only gave a nod and bowed his head. There was a moment of hesitation, and then Abishur said, "The two of you go on! Othniel, you know the way."

"Where are you going? What are you going to do?" Othniel asked.

"I had not thought about the consequence of Massoud's evil until now. We elders have allowed that monster to go to battle. And because of our fear, many innocent will suffer."

Abishur began to walk away when Melchior called out to him, "What could you possibly hope to do to make right the wrong that Massoud has done?"

Abishur stared intently at the two men and could only reply, "Faith. Courage. I guess I have a place for them after all, and the time for them seems to be now. May God bless you and give you speed."

And with that, the elder was gone, and, after a brief hesitation, Othniel and Melchior made good their escape.

CHAPTER TWENTY TWO

◆ ✚ ◆

The morning broke to a breathtaking scene. Emerging from the north side of the encampment were scores of mounted warriors bearing various weapons of death and destruction. Over one hundred of the camp's young and bitter had come to answer Massoud's call with or without their elders' blessings. Leading the 'war party' were Massoud's four remaining allies among the elders. Although a bit shaken by the magus' words, Falah, Akiva, Amoz and Davin were still loyal to Massoud to the end. Joining them out front were Moshae and Thanor, the renegade sons. They brought with them a good portion of their respective clans.

Three of the elders that had supported Massoud in the beginning, Bononi, El'hanan and Caled, were absent. However, Massoud had quickly replaced them with allies he had most prudently made within each of their clans. Bononi's youngest brother, Madaan, was more than eager to join the fray. He was a hot-tempered sort with no love lost on the foreigners. Madaan would gladly soak his sword with their blood. Talhah was El'hanan's grandson. The two had come to great disagreements over the running of the clan's many resources, and Talhah would gladly take this opportunity to wrestle control of the clan from the old man. And, finally, Caled's nephew, Elishama, led the renegades of his clan to follow Massoud, despite the elder's resistance. It seems Elishama still blames Caled for his father's death and would gladly supplant him as payback.

Massoud emerged from the left flank, adorned like a true Arabian king, sword in hand. The sight of their leader caused the expectant army to shout as one voice in a continued victory song. This brought a smile to Massoud's face as he realized his time had come and the battle was at hand. He rode toward the present and future clan leaders with a bit of pride. *Here,* he thought, *is the leadership that will build my coming empire! An empire in which the people will soon forget the name of my father, Barak, and turn their adoration upon me. My conquest that began amongst these renegades will be furthered by my victory over those Hebrews! And soon, I will ascend to the former power of my forefathers and take back all of the territory my father gave away!*

Intoxicated by the mere thought of such a massive conquest, Massoud became lost in a fantasy he was determined to bring to fruition, no matter what the cost. Unfortunately, upon closely inspecting his 'generals,' he remembered that, although nine clans were represented here, the other four clans were conspicuously absent. Try as he might, he could find no allies among those people, and yet, they were not here to oppose him. *No matter,* he thought, *their clans will be of no importance after my victory! They will be mere peasants, laborers in the building of my kingdom!*

This thought brought the smile back to his face as he approached Falah, his second-in-command, for his reports.

"All stand ready for your orders, Massoud!" Falah barked like a good soldier, "Over one hundred men have been counted in the young -- the strong -- ready to go into battle!"

Massoud came closer to Falah, "Very good. And what of our 'escaped' prisoners?"

"It seems, sir, that two or three were seen headed to Muza upon camels and another moving north quite fast on horseback. Shall we pursue and capture them, sir?"

Massoud looked toward the north and replied, "I have two or three men posted already to the north of us. That should slow the messenger down a bit. And, as for those headed to Muza, let them go."

Falah looked a bit shocked, "But, sir, the supposed successor to Barak's place of leadership is among them. Surely, we must destroy the child in order to solidify your place as our true leader!"

Massoud gave his second-in-command an indignant stare and said simply, "I need not worry about the child for long. I have also made preparations in Muza for such a time as this."

Suddenly, a rider interrupted the two coming in at full gallop. After catching his breath, the messenger reported, "The magus has escaped just as you supposed. Shall we intercept?"

Massoud's smile returned as his plans began to solidify into reality. "No! As I was saying, I have prepared a welcoming party for the magus and his 'friends.' Once they arrive in Muza, I will never need to give any of them a second thought."

Upon the high place, they could see the whole army -- sons, grandsons, brothers and nephews, their kin -- going into battle in an unjust war. The five who stand here now, were the same who stood in opposition to this war in the first place. Ariel, Jared, Hananel, Eben, and Kadam, all stood defenseless and speechless before the would-be conquerors. Some breathed prayers. Others pleaded to deaf ears for all of this to stop.

As the marching horde continued to move out of sight, some of the elders fell to their knees, unsure of the future. None of them dared break the silence. What words could possibly express the horror each and every one of them were feeling now? The time of talking was over anyway! They had lost the chance to stop this long ago and now stood with no visible recourse. Suddenly, they were awakened from their stupor by approaching footsteps.

As they all turned, the large form of Abishur appeared upon the top of the walkway that came from the camp. Following him were two very strong men of his clan, leading the largest bullock any of them had ever seen. The two strained to make the last step, and then laid the bullock upon the altar that had apparently fallen into disuse.

Abishur approached the holy ground reverently, taking his sandals off and prostrating himself in prayer. Behind him were three others who were even more hesitant to step upon the holy ground. But, after making reverent gestures, they too found their places behind Abishur, prostrate -- praying to the Almighty Living God. The other five weren't sure how to react. These three who had come with Abishur were all elders who had sided with Massoud. All of this was practically *their* fault! Their anger subsided as Abishur stood and spoke on the others' behalf, "Come brothers, the time for animosity is over. If we are to save our people, we must act now! Come quickly, we have much to repent of."

The ride had almost become too much for him. Stephanus had been taught endurance by delivering messages on horseback between Roman towns. But, that seemed like child's play compared to the grueling, uncaring desert that now surrounded him. His horse that began the journey strong and unwavering had now slowed considerably. Then, just as it seemed he and his horse would fall in exhaustion, Stephanus spotted a well sheltered in the hills. He made an immediate bee-line for the water and quickly drew enough for the both of them.

The wind had picked up quite a bit. Stephanus had not really noticed how much until he sat in the shelter of the rocks. Visibility had become almost nil. It seemed that a monster wind storm was beginning to take over the hill country.

I will never make it if this wind persists. But I must, he thought to himself. *I have to be getting close. I have been following the hill country all morning. There cannot be much further to go!*

He forced himself to his feet, still feeling a bit weak. Straining to mount the uncooperative horse, Stephanus fought to hold on. After several attempts, he realized that the horse was unwilling to go back into the wind storm. And who could blame him? Stephanus dismounted, took a water skin from the horse's gear, and turned to finish the journey on foot. It was then that he realized he was not alone.

CHAPTER TWENTY THREE

◆ ✚ ◆

A s the day wore on, their anxiety grew. Micaiah never sat anywhere for long, tending rather to pace around the others. The four of them, including Samuel, had set up camp just outside of Muza and now waited in nervous anticipation of the others. Azariah had retired early, resting in the shade of a nearby tree. Cala had found another shade in which she coaxed little Samuel off to sleep.

Micaiah tried his best to see in the distance for any sign of their friends, but they had unfortunately set up camp at the wrong side of a hill. Finally, filled with impatience and frustration, Micaiah spoke, "I am going to the top of the hill to look."

Cala cut him off, trying hard not to wake Samuel, "Again? This has to be the hundredth time, you know!"

Her brother sulled up, crossing his arms. He knew the pacing was doing him no good, but he was the type of person who had to do something! Trying his best to stay still, Micaiah began tapping his foot and looking around nervously. Finally, Cala could take no more. "Ok, go on then," she scolded.

Without hesitating, he turned and marched up the hill. Their temporary camp was beside the usual route, leading east out of the city, and they had watched many travelers pass this way today. And they could usually hear the noise of the coming caravans approaching the top of the hill. So, imagine Micaiah's surprise when he was met at the top of the hill by a pair of mounted travelers.

Stephanus was stopped completely, frozen in his tracks. Two looming figures were entering the shelter of the rocks, fleeing the coming storm. Both were leading camels and both were covered from head to toe in cloth. Neither had noticed the boy yet as they began to make themselves comfortable.

Stephanus stepped back to the horse to retrieve a small knife that Othniel had given him. He had forgotten it before, but suddenly found use for it. Unfortunately, the horse thought he was about to be forced out into the storm and decided to fight this notion with everything he had in him. This commotion drew the attention of the two strangers, who then whirled around to face Stephanus with their staffs ready for combat.

Once he was able to see their faces, he realized that these were not Massoud's men unless the wretch had taken a liking to Hebrews, and that was not likely. This changed everything! Stephanus relaxed and forgot about the knife again. He had made it, and now he could relay the urgent message. The only problem was there was nobody to tell the two Hebrews that everything was all right. They seemed a bit on edge if not all out unfriendly toward this foreign stranger they had happened upon. Stephanus suddenly began to doubt if they had made the right decision in sending him.

Massoud had never thought that war could be so difficult to orchestrate or that a hundred men could move so slowly. The end of the day was approaching and they were only half way there. It was obvious that they would need to make camp very soon and prepare to rest for the battle to come. It was the last thing Massoud wanted to do, but, unfortunately, it was the most prudent choice they had. Still, he felt the need to push them as far as possible so as to be ready to strike as early as possible.

His scouts had not returned to report and this was beginning to bother him. They were his eyes to the north, and without them, he and his army were literally running blind into battle. Not smart. But still, he pressed forward. They needed to go far enough to shorten the campaign tomorrow, and, yet, they needed to stay far enough away so as not to tip their hand. So how far was too far, and how close was too close? Such decisions to be made! And yet, they did have to be made.

He had just done a bit of mental 'weights and measures,' weighing the pros and cons of the possibilities set before him, when a horseman was spotted coming south at great speed. It was hard to see the approaching rider, for, although the sun was still up, the wind was making it quite difficult to see ahead.

There was a tense moment. Massoud signaled halt! And, then, it was confirmed. The rider was one of theirs! Coming down from a full gallop, the scout whirled around to face his leader. From the look on his face, it wasn't good news.

"To the north, from all directions, the storm blocks our path! It would be suicide to continue. We must . . ."

Massoud gave the horseman a glare that kept him from finishing as Massoud continued the rider's sentence, "We must what? Flee? Run? Retreat? Why is it that there are so many of you so willing to cower to the slightest thing?" Massoud looked to his generals. "We will make camp in the cleft of the hills to the north. There we will wait out this storm overnight. By tomorrow, it will be gone, and we will still be here!"

The messenger gathered every bit of courage he had and replied, "My lord, I do not think you understand! This is no ordinary storm! The winds have gathered together from the four corners of the world and they have created a beast of a storm that has begun to tear across the hill country. We may not be able to escape, even now!"

"Escape? You speak as if we are facing warriors in battle here, or an angry animal that will surely devour us. No, it is only a storm and we will wait . . .it . . ."

Suddenly, from the north, a sound of a million chariots charging raged and echoed against the hills. Massoud, for once, was found speechless before what his eyes could not deny. Even through zero visibility, all present could see what was coming. A remarkable wave of cloud, smoke and dirt towered over the warriors, leaving them for a moment frozen in fear. It seemed to reach to the heavens themselves and no end was seen to its width. Every rider suddenly could feel the ground tremble before the windstorm to end all windstorms.

Some began to utter prayers, both silent and spoken. Most realized that it was much too late.

CHAPTER TWENTY FOUR

◆ ✚ ◆

T he sound was heard throughout the hill country, even as far
as Muza. No one was quite sure what it was, but many had
an idea of what it meant. Abishur had just finished properly
portioning the sacrificed bullock according to the scriptures and had
begun to burn the proper parts when the sound reached his ears. All
present heard it too and came to their feet. The sun at first seemed
to be setting, but upon a second glance, it was clear that something
was blotting the sun out. After a third and fourth look, the elders
spotted it. A monstrous sand storm was coming from the north,
shaking even the high place. It rolled like a huge wave on the ocean,
and it was headed straight for the encampment below.

One by one, the weakened form of each and every elder was
forced to kneel in the presence of the divine wrath of their angered
God. All quickly found voice enough to call out to the God of
their fathers for one last petition. Abishur focused his attention
mainly upon the sacrifice, finishing the fine points. As the fire began
to consume the bullock parts and the smoke rose amazingly to
the skies, defying the persistent north wind, all present witnessed
something truly amazing.

As the smoke from the sacrifice reached the heavens, the storm that threatened to consume them all faded into non-existence. It left behind only a strong north wind passing through the encampment and the high place without consequence. God had heard them and spared them in divine mercy. After a few moments, the whole camp finally caught their breaths and realized the storm had passed them by. Suddenly, there was an eruption of voices from all corners of the camp. The elders stared in awe as Barak's people were giving thanks from deep within their very souls.

Abishur was as awestruck as any. When the wind had blown through the high place, the elder had ceased his sacrifice and had turned to face the storm. When he turned back to the sacrifice, he was even more amazed. The bullock had been consumed.

Othniel was as surprised as Micaiah to meet so suddenly at the crest of the hill. Both were still a bundle of nerves and so much so that they nearly attacked one another out of base reflexes. There was a fleeting moment of embracing and welcoming one another, and then a quick mounting of their animals and, then, off to Muza.

Melchior, weary of traveling already, found the sight of the port city more welcoming than ever. There had been times within the last week that he was sure he would never return home, and there were also times that he could not have cared less either way. But, now that he was actually returning, by the grace of the living God above, he was glad.

There had been no word from Stephanus and that worried the magus. To send the boy into such danger, to a land he knew nothing about, to warn a people he could hardly communicate with, seemed a bit chancy. But the deed was done! And besides, the favor and care of God Himself seemed to be with them thus far. There was no reason to doubt now!

The small party made its way through busy streets, trying desperately to hurry. But the size of the crowd made haste impossible. Melchior could see the heights of his observatory peaking over the other buildings, getting closer by the minute, and this comforted him greatly. He found himself clutching something hidden in his cloak quite affectionately. He hadn't realized it before, but he had been caressing the fine jar of myrrh given to him by Barak ever since they left the encampment. It was all he had left to remember his friend. It was his only anchor to sanity in a world that seemed to have been turned upside down. It became the only thing he could actually focus on -- as if the only path his future could follow was to fulfill the request of a dying friend. And seeing the observatory made it that much clearer. The star!

As much as his weary frame would like to have contemplated a long rest, his spirit knew the truth. All his life had been preparation and rehearsal for this moment. Everything he knew, everyone he had loved and learned from, every experience, every scroll, and every star had brought him here. And, as he embraced the flask of myrrh, he knew what had to be done next.

But how? Such a journey would be costly and dangerous. The weather was not always kind, and the many city-states were constantly at war. Melchior no longer knew anyone who worked the caravan routes, and the seas were ruled by storms and pirates. Surely, there was another way. For a man of Melchior's advanced years to venture a journey from Muza to Jerusalem would be suicide . . .suicide.

Melchior's train of thought was suddenly broken by a ghastly sight. Stopping his camel quite suddenly, he found he could only stare. And since the elder was leading the way through a narrow alley opening, his sudden stop caught everyone's attention. Following Melchior's frozen stare, all eyes looked to the skyline just ahead of them. Just over the next set of buildings rose the majesty of his sanctum, the observatory. All eyes became fixed upon it, not due to awe or wonder, but shock and horror. Billowing out of every opening was the blackest of smoke, and tongues of burning fire!

CHAPTER TWENTY FIVE

❖ ✚ ❖

L uckily, Stephanus knew a bit of the Hebrews language that his Father had taught him (it was one of the dialects his Father had championed when preparing for his mission) and was able to convince the two Hebrews that he was a friend, and that what he was saying was important. It had not been quite as hard to communicate with them as he had first supposed, but it became harder and harder to ease their suspicion concerning this unwelcome foreigner who had "invaded" the southern edge of their land. Even invoking the names of Barak and Azariah did nothing to win them over. It was especially difficult to get them to understand anything else once they were told of Johan'an's death.

Johan'an was apparently as important to the Hebrews as Barak had been to the herdsmen to the south. His death left a great void of leadership which would affect their people for another generation or so. But that is another story.

These two Hebrews were scouts. There had been reports of an armed force moving toward them from the south. And, although the very thought seemed ludicrous, it would have been foolish to ignore the possibility. And, now, every word that Stephanus uttered confirmed the reports.

The storm had moved quickly to the south and quietly disappeared. Once clear, the three of them quickly mounted up and left the safety of the rocks surrounding the well. They were joined by about ten others, and, instead of heading north to safety, all of them began to bear south to spy out the size of the coming war force.

There were still signs that the others were uncertain about Stephanus and his story; cold stares, side comments he didn't even try to decipher; and, from time to time, one of them would search his belongings, looking for some sign of deceit. Othniel's knife raised a few eyebrows, but before long they eased down a bit.

The storm had died down, revealing a setting sun. Stephanus began to wonder where Massoud and his hundred man army were. Had they turned back? Was the storm too much for even them? Had they stopped to camp for the night? Or were they just over that raised dune up ahead waiting to ambush them?

The longer this trip went on, the more worried and fearful Stephanus became. The Hebrew party had increased to at least twenty five now, but they were still no match for Massoud's forces. He had tried many times to voice this concern, but found no voice to do so. It seemed that he was as unsure as to what his traveling mates' reactions would be as the Hebrews were of his motives. So they continued on in silence, awaiting what may lay over the next horizon.

There were quite a few horizons to go over. So many that Stephanus was sure that every turn they made would put them face to face with that fiend, Massoud. But it was beginning to look like a lost cause, and Stephanus wasn't sure he was sorry. Then over that one particular horizon came a sight Stephanus never forgot, even to his old age.

Back in Muza, Melchior had broken his stare and took off like a shot. His speed and sudden departure left the others gawking motionless at the blazing inferno. Othniel, of course, was the first to notice his master's absence and called to the others as he sped off after the elder magus. The alleys and streets ahead had suddenly become crowded with people fleeing the sight of the burning sanctum. Muza was a wonderful place to live, but in times such as these, it always seemed that it was every man for himself.

Cala was bringing up the rear of the group and seemed to be falling a bit behind. She couldn't take her eyes off the burning observatory that still peaked over the buildings between her and the inferno. It appeared that the more frantically the small group tried to fight through the crowd, the thicker and harder it was to make a way against the flow of people. Cala was more taken with the sight blazing over the skyline that she was fighting the crowd. Of equal concern to her was her newborn son. Young Samuel had seen too much action for his age, and should be resting instead of being jostled through the city streets like a sack of goods.

Micaiah kept one eye on Cala and another on this grandfather, Azariah, who had pushed ahead after Othniel. Soon it was a lost cause to look for the elder. The crowds, although beginning to thin, were still a bit bothersome. Now the day's light was beginning to fade. He decided that since he could still see his sister, Cala, he should concern himself more with her safety.

Othniel was now moving as fast as he possibly could. He could no longer see his master but, fortunately, the crowd was beginning to part to keep from being trampled by the eager servant's horse. It was a good thing he knew these streets so well, for the shortest route had now become a necessity. The giant turned his horse with a great deal of effort to an empty alleyway. The maneuver had proven to be difficult and reminded Othniel of how much he hated horses.

Once in the alleyway, Othniel pushed his horse to a full gallop, for just ahead, at the other end, he could see his master, Melchior. Unfortunately, he was not alone.

Although it was growing quite dark, in the direct background the sanctum was burning brightly, showing the scene before Othniel quite plainly. His master was surrounded by about six or seven men, all cloaked and hooded. Melchior seemed to be fending them all off single-handedly. But at a closer look, they were simply toying with the old man, knowing that he was no match for any of them. This angered Othniel a great deal, and, in reaction, he pushed the horse even faster and gave what sounded like a war cry.

Melchior's assailants stopped to greet the incoming threat, drawing their swords and returning the cry. But, as Othniel exited the alley, he felt the strike of a staff hit him across the chest, dismounting him. As the giant hit the ground with a thunderous blow, and yet he instinctively reached for his knife. He suddenly realized that he had given Stephanus his weapon of choice. This left him defenseless as the swordsmen pinned him to the ground.

There was nothing Othniel could do but stare angrily at the faces of his captors. There was a moment he was sure he would die, but he was certainly not giving these fiends the satisfaction of seeing him beg or plead. Ready to accept death with honor and courage, he awaited the inevitable. His only thought was for the safety of his master and friend, Melchior. Suddenly, the thought welled up within him, *How could I possibly give in to death without a fight if it might mean my master could escape with his life?* This thought brought him more courage as he prepared to fight to the end. Then, suddenly, Othniel felt the coldness of a blade come against his throat. The others scattered as the one holding the sword knelt down by the giant's side.

At first, it was impossible to see his enemy's face. But as the rogue knelt closer, the firelight revealed a familiar sinister smile.

"What did I tell you, old friend? Are not our paths destined to cross again and again and again? And here we are again!"

The voice of the cutthroat Bassam broke into a hideous laugh as the sanctum continued to burn.

Chapter Twenty Six

❖ ✚ ❖

The darkness slowly made its way over the hill country and steadily took over the sky. Most of the Hebrew scouts had lit torches, which flickered off the hills like writhing ghosts. This made the scene before Stephanus even more ominous and foreboding, and left the boy speechless and unwilling to go on. But after receiving a few nudges from his "escort," Stephanus continued forward.

For as far as the light carried and to all directions, the ground seemed to be littered with what was left of Massoud's army. Horses, camels, and men half-buried in the sand looked more like the statues Stephanus had seen in the temples or the stone carvings adorning many of the halls, libraries, and arenas all over Rome. There was no apparent order to the army. All seemed to have been fleeing for what was left of their lives. Most were turned away from the storm and toward the south -- caught in mid-retreat. But this attempt to flee was apparently futile.

Upon a closer look Stephanus could see the expression upon every ill-fated face. Eyes wide with horror; hands raised in an attempt to hold off the storm; weapons cast aside useless; mouths mysteriously open in either a final scream or one last plea for their God's mercy.

The Hebrew scouts busied themselves looking for survivors, but the search proved useless. There was a great deal of speculation and discussion, but Stephanus was too preoccupied to follow the talk. He was too busy wondering to himself whether this was all a bit of sad irony or possibly the wrath of these Hebrews' God protecting them from harm. He had studied the God of Jerusalem, briefly. His teacher had taught it like some children's fantasy or a primitive, outdated myth. To believe in only one God when the world was full of gods -- it all seemed a bit too much to accept. But looking upon the faces of every would-be warrior, their features twisted in horror, all the stories of slain giants, parted seas, walls crumbling and this Yahweh, revealing himself to a chosen nation upon a thunderous mountain, began to sound a bit more believable.

After what seemed like a lifetime, Stephanus found himself along the hind-most ranks of the army. They were still in no particular order. In fact, the farther to the rear he got, the more chaotic the statuesque army seemed to be arranged. He had seen the battles of men against men upon the fields of valor, the blood and bodies covering the expanse of the battle zone. But he had never seen so many men massacred by a force of nature. No god he had ever read about seemed ready to lift his or her hands against a people in such a way as this. What kind of god was this that was willing to manifest himself in such ways and judge men so? Stephanus wasn't quite sure he wanted to find out -- yet there was something about Melchior that drew him near -- a side to the old man's God that intrigued him.

Suddenly, thoughts of the magus brought Stephanus back around. Turning back toward the "army," a flood of horror rushed against his already beleaguered mind. He had looked into the faces of almost every warrior and yet, something, or someone, was missing. The realization weighed heavily upon the young Roman, almost causing him to faint. His stagger caught the attention of a couple of the Hebrews who rushed to brace him up. Looking deep into their concerned eyes, all he could manage to say was, "Massoud . . ."

Although Bassam's sword was pressing harder and harder against Othniel's jugular, the giant was sure the cut-throat's laugh would kill him first. The pain of his dismount was almost unbearable. But that laugh . . . was just too much.

Melchior had found himself, once again, struggling with Bassam's men. The cut-throats couldn't imagine why, if the old man was so wise, he insisted on trying to escaping from them toward the burning building. The elder guessed if any of these vagrant menaces ever had anything that vaguely resembled a home, they would know. They would understand. But they didn't. Or they couldn't.

To Melchior, it was as if his heart was melting in the heat of the fire. The magus' emotions ran from one extreme to another, from hopelessness to pure rage, leaving the hooded thieves wondering what the old man would do next. Melchior could see into the sanctum and even more clearly into the library itself. And, although he could see the main table serving as kindling to the fire, he could also see the walls lined with scroll upon scroll -- scrolls that were filled with precious, holy words. He struggled once again to break free, pulling the thugs toward the burning sanctum door, with every ounce of strength his aged body could muster.

"Bassam!" called out one of the struggling thugs, "What are we to do with this old man?"

Bassam, never skipping a beat, simply said, "Our orders were to kill them all. That is what we are being paid to do, and that is definitely what we are going to do!"

Othniel's eyes grew wider and his soul sank as he repeated, "Kill . . ."

Bassam looked down upon the face of the giant and said with a bit of scorn, "Yes, kill . . . Kill them all! Why are you so surprised, oaf! Do you not believe me capable of such a thing?"

Othniel, a bit red-faced and growing redder by the minute, gave a tense smile, "No! Surprised, I am not! In fact, in the long run I quite expected it, but if it is gold or silver that truly motivates you, why settle for a nugget when you can have the whole blasted mine?"

Bassam's smile changed a bit as he knelt quite close to Othniel's face and said, "Oh, my boy, it is quite a lot more then silver and gold . . .Oh, it is much more than that. In fact, I could say it is rather a personal thing, would you not agree?"

The cut-throat's sword pressed a little harder, and his smile turned a bit sour as he continued, "And why make deals for the mine when you can own the whole flaming mountain?!"

Bassam's blade began digging into the skin and Othniel found himself helpless to his apparent fate. Then, suddenly, a camel and rider darted from the darkness nearly running over Bassam, his cut-throats, and Othniel all in the process.

Bassam dropped his sword while attempting to save his own skin, and Othniel suddenly found himself free and within reach of a weapon. One of Bassam's men had not been so lucky. Having been struck by the charging camel, he was left with a rather nasty gash in the side of his head. The others had all jumped to safety, while a couple of the others had managed to apprehend the camel rider.

Had Othniel been looking, he would have seen that the rider was indeed the elder Azariah. The charge had taken a great deal out of him, which left him easy prey for Bassam's cut-throats. They were attempting to dismount the old man when another rider appeared in full gallop. When the new assailant reached Azariah, he leaped from his camel onto the elder's attackers. It was, of course, Micaiah who had come to his grandfather's rescue, which led Melchior to wonder where dear Cala and the child, Samuel, were.

Othniel was much too busy to pay the others any attention whatsoever. He found himself on one knee, reaching for Bassam's sword. The grinning cut-throat was within pouncing distance. Their eyes were locked, each awaiting the others move. The severely injured thug lay close to his leader, sword clutched in a death grip. For the longest time, it was a true stand-off. And, then, they both went for a weapon.

Othniel happened to get his hands on Bassam's sword before the villain could even get close. But Bassam had already realized this and attempted to take the sword from his dying mate. Unfortunately, the thug had already passed on to whatever fate awaited him and was rather unwilling to give up the sword. Suddenly, Othniel struck without warning or mercy. Bassam gave a frantic, spastic jump to the side, barely escaping his own blade, and then began to desperately fight for the dead man's sword. In the meantime, he also began calling to the others for help or a sword to no avail. Grabbing the hilt and blade, being careful not to cut himself in the process, Bassam gave a powerful twist, breaking most of the fingers on the dead man's hand, while using the limp sword arm to block Othniel's savage attack. Finally, the sword was free and the two enemies circled each other like hungry wolves.

Suddenly, the battle was interrupted by a cry from one of Bassam's men, "The old magician got away, Bassam!"

At this, it was Othniel who smiled and Bassam, unwilling to break eye contact, yelled back, "Well, go after him, you idiot! That is our payday!"

There was a great deal of hesitation and uncertainty in the voice that answered, "Pay day or no pay day, no way I am going into that fire!"

Othniel turned to the voice in horror as the thug just stood there pointing into the burning sanctum. The smoke billowed out of every opening and the heat was becoming unbearable. He could see Azariah and Micaiah held and bound with ropes, but his master, Melchior was nowhere in sight.

CHAPTER TWENTY-SEVEN

◆ ✚ ◆

Turning away from Bassam almost proved to be a fatal mistake. For, as soon as Othniel turned to look for his master, the cut-throat viciously attacked without a bit of warning. Luckily, Micaiah saw the attack coming and warned his friend with a shout. Dodging to the right, the gentle giant escaped with only a cut across his left arm. Unfortunately, the cut was deep and painful.

Othniel grabbed his aching, bleeding arm. Suddenly, Bassam struck again, almost landing a deathly lunge to the heart. Othniel was able to turn and block with the sword which had begun to slip around in his blood-soaked hand. With every blow, Othniel lost more and more ground. He now found himself sprawled out upon the ground trying desperately to block Bassam's attacks.

Micaiah was unable to give Othniel any help whatsoever. His hands were bound and the thugs held him and his grandfather at knife-point, never taking their eyes off of the two of them. The young Hebrew had been in this position too much lately. He was a man of power, a man of action, a warrior. And for him to be disarmed, bound and helpless, was almost too much for his sanity.

Othniel had backed up opposite of the sanctum's front door. Pulling up on the wall, he could still feel the heat of the fire. To think that his master was inside drove him to the brink of a berserk rage. Slashing wildly, he only walked into every trap the grinning cut-throat set before him. Suddenly, the giant tripped and fell back against the wall, dropping his sword. Bassam's blade resumed its prior position close to Othniel's already bleeding neck.

"So, this is the way it ends, eh, old friend? I was paid to set you free so long ago, and now I am paid to end your sorry existence. Strange, fate's sense of humor, eh?"

But Othniel refused to answer. Instead, he gave the fiend a brave stare and spit on his shoes as a final, indignant curse. The cut-throat never broke his smile, as he looked down at his stained boots and then back at Othniel.

"Oh, good shot, Othniel! I will just have to take some of that gold I found in the sanctum to buy me a new pair, eh? Well, as far as that goes, I could buy most of Muza new boots. Ha!"

He had broken out in that hideous laugh again, unfortunately, and Othniel began to wonder how many of Bassam's victors had died with that sickening sound ringing in their ears. Calming down to a chuckle, he continued, "Any last words before I do the deed?"

Othniel was unwilling to play the evil one's game and would only lift his eyes to the heavens above to send one last prayer up for his dear master.

Suddenly, a voice spoke from the darkness of the alleyway just behind Bassam. "The Lord saith *"What the wicked dreads will overtake him . . . When the storm has swept by, the wicked one is gone!"*

Bassam spun around with the speed and agility of a great cat only to be met with a ferocious punch to the head. The cut-throat fell unconscious upon the ground, lying out in an odd sort of way, having blacked out long before he hit the ground. A dark figure stepped out of the blackness and stood over Bassam and continued, *"The fear of the Lord adds length to life, but the years of the wicked are cut short! The Lord has thus spoken, let it be so!"*

Before Bassam's men could react, they found themselves surrounded, outnumbered, and held at sword-point. The dark figure stepped out into the open area. The fire reflected off the stranger's clothes from head to toe. His eyes cut through the dark like the moon on a clear night. Looking around, his deep, authoritative voice rang out once again, "Where is he that is called Melchior? I have come a great distance and I seek the wise one's council."

Suddenly, Othniel, Azariah, and Micaiah in unison turned toward the burning sanctum, all realizing the magus was still inside.

Melchior had made it into the library. Although almost overcome by the heat, the magus was unwilling to let his life's work go up in flames. Frantically, he began to pull the scrolls, which had survived thus far, off the wall and into his tunic. But, no matter how hard he tried, inevitably a scroll or two, or even three, would slip out of his hands and into the fire which threatened to consume him.

He had turned to the far wall, intending to continue, but was suddenly overtaken by the smoke. The coughing fit that ensued made his whole body convulse, nearly throwing the elder to the ground. Suddenly, dizzy from the violent wheezing and gasping, Melchior lost his balance. Finding nothing to brace himself on that wasn't already burning, the magus fell hard to the floor, and this time Othniel wasn't there to catch him.

Trying hard to retain his consciousness, Melchior fought to pull himself back up to no avail. His body screamed in pain from inside to out, and he couldn't tell which felt worse -- the pain in his hip where he fell, or the agony of his gasping lungs. Suddenly, he realized most of the scrolls he had picked up had dropped across the floor when he fell. In a desperate frenzy, Melchior attempted to gather them back to him, only to burn his hands many times and ended up watching them burn without hope of ever recovering them.

Finally, the old man fell back, bracing himself against the wall and watching his life literally burn up before his eyes. All the work he had done, the eternal quest for knowledge and truth, was being consumed, leaving him no alternative but to prepare to meet his God. No matter how tragic the end seemed to him, he couldn't help but think how fitting it all was. Ready to pass to the other side, ready to stand before a holy God and answer for his life, and find, in the end, all the things he had done and all the knowledge he had acquired were firewood before the wisdom and holiness of God.

Finding it hard to breathe, Melchior relaxed and smiled and recited under his breath an old psalm, "Yes, I am always with you. You hold me by my right hand. You guide me with your counsel and, afterward, you will take me into glory . . ."

As he began to close his eyes one final time, he caught a glimpse of something shimmering and flickering in the fire. He watched it a bit longer when suddenly the shimmering took an almost human form. And then there were two forms stepping through the fire coming toward him. His eyes grew wide and his arms reached to embrace the figures coming toward him as he whispered under his breath, "Behold, the angels of the Lord . . ."

And, with that, he passed out.

When Melchior came to again, instead of light, he mostly saw darkness. He could still see some of the shimmering effect he had witnessed earlier, but the figures around him were no longer shining so fiercely in the fire. They were darker, more mundane. One of the figures had knelt beside him and seemed to be tending to some burns and bruises the magus was suffering. Melchior could tell this mainly because every once in a while, the figure would press on a tender spot and pain would race through his body.

This was the first sign that he wasn't dead. Melchior began coughing and heaving violently, which brought a few of the other figures to his side. One of them brought something wet and cool to his lips and encouraged him to drink. Suddenly, as his vision began to clear, he noticed the rings of gold on the hand that served him. The other hand had been placed behind his head to brace the elder as he drank. Then, Melchior came eye-to-eye with his benefactor.

The man before him was indeed a far bit darker-skinned than the native residents of Muza or the hill country. He was a young man with stern and rigid features, although the moment they gained eye contact, the man's features softened considerably. The man was wearing a headdress unfamiliar to Melchior, but the old magus was sure he had seen it somewhere. His neck was adorned with all sorts of golden jewelry, as were his hands, and his tunic, which hung to his knees. He was covered in golden metal plates. He carried a walking stick made of a knotted, twisted wood. And across his shoulders and along his back hung the skin of a jaguar or a puma -- Melchior couldn't be quite sure at this point which it was.

Looking up into the face of the young foreigner, Melchior saw expressions he was accustomed to seeing upon his servant Othniel's face -- something akin to respect and honor. Although the two had never met, it was as though the young man had spent all his years at Melchior's side. When the foreigner realized that the elder magus had revived, he began to speak, "I am Balthazar of Ethiopia. Are you Melchior, the wise and holy man of Muza?"

Melchior gathered his breath and his strength, and replied, "I am the man you search for. Do I have you to thank for saving my life?"

As Melchior awaited an answer, he could have sworn this young Bathazar was shedding a tear. There was a pause, and then, as he took the elder's hand in his, he continued, almost ceremoniously, "I, Balthazar, seventh son of a seventh son, descendant of the royal linage of Melinik, he who is called Ebna-Hakim, or *'son of the wise one,'* born of the royal line of the seed of sacred Makeda, queen of Sheba, and Wise Solomon, great king of Israel. I now place myself and my company at your most honorable disposal . . ."

As the young foreigner bowed his head in respect, Melchior could only say, "I am sorry. . . I do not understand."

At this answer, the young foreigner looked up from his reverent position with an astonished look. He seemed to be speechless, unwilling to accept the reply. And then he *had* to speak, "I am afraid, oh wise one, I am the one who does not understand . . ." Balthazar hesitated, grasping for the words, "You cannot tell me you did not see it?"

Melchior, still breathing unevenly, could only return a puzzled look. Bathazar, gasping in unbelief, went on, "You had to have seen it! It is unfathomable to think that you could have missed it! Even an amateur would have noticed . . ."

Finally, realizing Melchior had no idea what he was talking about, he blurted, "Are you telling me you did not see the star?"

Suddenly, Melchior's smoke-weary eyes grew wide as he found himself repeating, "The star!"

EPILOGUE ONE

· ✦ ·

The sobering realization that Massoud was not among the dead left Stephanus looking over his shoulder and jumping at every shadow that moved in the desert. He, like everyone, knew what to expect from the demon, and, now, he would be desperate and full of rage. The two Hebrews that had been chosen to escort the young Roman back to Barak's encampment had learned to trust the young boy. Maybe they were too busy replaying the horror they had just seen in their heads over and over again or maybe they finally saw him as no threat. Whatever it was, it was good to not have to worry about his fate at the hands of these men, at least. But, until he reached the safety of the camp, he wasn't about to relax.

The Hebrews muttered to themselves in a broken Aramaic that Stephanus had a hard time following. True, his Father had him trained in the neighboring dialects. But this version was different, rougher. It smacked of the Jews he had come into contact with in Egypt. Which stood to reason. After all, according to Azaraiah, they claimed their lineage, like Melchior, from their self proclaimed 'Promised Land.' Not that Stephanus had any reason to doubt their conviction.

They were moving at a moderate pace now. Word had to be passed on to Barak's people no matter how much it would devastate them. Many of their young died following Massoud. It would take time to heal the wounds of the past few days and for any of them to move on.

MOVE ON.

That thought ran through Stephanus's mind like a Legionnaires' spear. What now? His Father is dead. His homeland is so far away. Even the outskirts of the Roman Territories seemed beyond his reach. And this mad holy man didn't seem to be any help. But the old man had lost so much; too much for a man of his station of life to bear. No, he had to play this through. Surely, once the smoked cleared, Melchior would help him to journey home. Right now, he had a message to deliver and a warning to give.

Suddenly, there was cry from behind them. All three slowed to a halt and turned to see a lone rider racing toward them. Behind the solitary horseman raged four others; thundering like a mythical holocaust. Before the incoming Hebrew could reach his brothers, one of the horsemen overcame him and ran him through with what looked like a scythe! Falling to the ground, the dying, young rider found himself trampled by the relentless pursuers.

Suddenly, the other two Hebrews pushed their horses into a full on run. Stephanus didn't hesitate to join them. The three of them sped away, hoping to leave the ghostly apparitions behind to no avail. One of the four attackers produced a bow with an arrow and quickly took one of the two Hebrews down with a perfect shot to the neck! As the body hit the ground, Stephanus and the remaining Hebrew pushed on as if their lives depended on it; because, it did.

Stephanus, being a better rider and lighter in the saddle, pulled ahead of his new companions. Though their horses were nearly exhausted, they seemed to understand the urgency of escaping the situation at hand. Stephanus felt himself pull ahead as he heard the other Hebrews fall to the ground. The hoof beats of the approaching marauders got closer and closer. It was now, more than ever, that the young Roman wished he had something or someone to cry to. As his fate was nearly sealed, he wished he could call on the gods of the Romans like Melchior called upon his God! But he never felt the presence of Jupiter or Ares in times of crises. And he had never seen any of his people's gods act in such a manner as this Hebrew God did.

Stephanus closed his eyes, nearly accepting his fate. As the hoof beats were upon him and the breath of the riders could be felt on his back, he called out in a manner he never had.

"God of Melchior, save me!"

He closed his eyes tight, expecting the worse and feeling the tiny bit of faith he had mustered disappear. He threw his hands out as if to accept his final end.

But there was none. Just silence. The horsemen had stopped. And, as Stephanus opened his eyes, he saw why. He had arrived at Barak's camp. Suddenly, at the edge of the encampment, he stopped and spun around. The four horsemen had stopped on the hill overlooking the place they had called home not long ago. The boy just stared in disbelief as another rider appeared and crossed in front of the other four. It was Massoud, he thought. Although, it was hard to tell. He was covered head to toe by cloth. But it was the eyes that gave him away. For, from the top of the hill, Stephanus could see the blazing eyes of Massoud peering from the cloth that covered his face.

After a short while, transfixed in the moment, the one thought to be Massoud drew his sword and held it high in a threatening manner. Stephanus knew what he would do with that sword given the chance and he wasn't about to allow that. The hand gripping the sword was naked to the sun and was white as alabaster almost dead and wretched. After a few passes, Massoud called his horsemen and they disappeared over the hill.

Stephanus let out a breath of relief and fell from his horse. He was safe, but for how long? Melchior and the others had to be warned. The whole hill country had to be warned. Massoud had survived and he wasn't finished. But, for a time, Stephanus would rest. But not for long.

Epilogue Two

◆ ✚ ◆

A nd to think he had almost given up.
The darkness had come so close to winning, so close to
burying him in his own pain and age. But, now, everything
had changed. Melchior found himself in the presence of one who
reminded the elder magus of himself, only a great many years
younger. His presence had made Melchior forget about his once
insurmountable frailty. Just being around the newcomer, Melchior
seemed injected with new life in his once slowing veins.

The soldiers who had come with Balthazar knew how to bind
wounds with precision accuracy. They had apparently had plenty of
practice on the field of battle. They weren't much on conversation,
though. They either didn't know the language or didn't care to try
and communicate at all. They just went about their work as though
they were expecting to go into battle soon. And, as far as that goes,
Othniel didn't doubt there weren't a few more wars just over the
horizon.

Melchior had become caught up with his new visitor. They had
been off to themselves ever since the fire in the sanctum had been
put out. Othniel couldn't help but dislike the stranger.

"More chattering about that star, " Othniel thought shuddering.

His elderly benefactor would no doubt be charged up and ready to head out after his mysterious star. And just when he was sure that Melchior had given up on that death march into oblivion.

Luckily, the elder wasn't paying attention to Othniel at the time or he could have read the young man's face easily. No, the magus was far too busy soaking up the fellowship of his younger, more eager colleague. They were both, just now, studying a map of the trade routes; plotting a route to the holy lands. There was no doubt in either of their voices as they chose a plan of action.

Balthazar wanted to leave immediately, but Melchior insisted that they had to go back to Barak's encampment and discover their fate. Balthazar reluctantly agreed as he began barking orders to his soldiers. They immediately jumped to attention at his every command, readying all for departure.

Meanwhile, Azariah, and Micaiah were eager to return to their people. Besides the fact that they wanted to find out the fate of their families back at the Hebrew encampment, they both wanted to make sure Cala was safe. They had succeeded at keeping her and Samuel out of harm's way. This was no time to let down their guard. Micaiah was unsure whether to trust the new arrivals, but for the time being he had no choice. He couldn't wait to get home, away from all of these strangers. It seemed it was venturing outside of their home encampment that got their father killed in the first place.

"Nothing good can come of following these two heathen sorcerers around!" Micaiah thought to himself, "Nothing."

Azariah, however, listened to the two magi with great eagerness. He didn't understand everything the two were saying, but it all had to do with his people's promised Messiah! So, of course, it piqued his interest.

Melchior sat in front of Balthazar with an unfamiliar smile on his face. It felt good. In fact, this whole situation felt, well, right! He sat there thinking of how God had been with him every step of the way; all the while, turning a scroll around in his aged hands.

"This was the only thing I was able to save from the fire." Melchior said, sadly. "All of my life's work gone. All of that work, wasted."

Balthazar reached out and touched the elder's hand, "Not wasted, Melchior. All of that was done to prepare you for your greatest journey. It was all a part of bringing you to your greatest of quests: the chance to see our King, our Messiah born!"

Their eyes locked, tears beginning to roll down the cheeks of the magi.

Melchior smiled through his tears and replied as he stood, "Yes. It is time for us to go. Time to see our God!"